"I'm at...

Then Gray felt it, ... between them wasn't just on her side, Eve thought.

"As you know, I've been married and have a daughter. It was never a happy marriage and I've learned my lesson. I'll never get seriously involved with a woman again."

Eve was totally confused. "I'm flattered," she said, "but what does all this have to do with whether or not I tutor your daughter?"

"For a while I thought it might not be a good idea to work closely with you, knowing there was this attraction for you on my part, but that's absurd," Gray said. "After all, you're a beautiful and charming woman. You no doubt have a lot of admirers."

Eve didn't know how to reply to that. Did Gray want her to be his daughter's tutor or his lover? Both? Or neither? Heaven knew she was attracted to him, too. And she wasn't any more eager to get involved with him than he was with her. No matter what he had in mind, he was making it clear it wasn't wedding bells, and she wouldn't accept anything less from any man....

Dear Reader,

September's stellar selections beautifully exemplify Silhouette Romance's commitment to publish strong, emotional love stories that touch every woman's heart. In *The Baby Bond*, Lilian Darcy pens the poignant tale of a surrogate mom who discovers the father knew nothing of his impending daddyhood! His demand: a marriage of convenience to protect their BUNDLES OF JOY....

Carol Grace pairs a sheik with his plain-Jane secretary in a marriage meant to satisfy family requirements. But the oil tycoon's shocked to learn that being *Married to the Sheik* is his VIRGIN BRIDE's secret desire.... FOR THE CHILDREN, Diana Whitney's miniseries that launched in Special Edition in August 1999—and returns to that series in October 1999—crosses into Silhouette Romance with *A Dad of His Own*, the touching story of a man, mistaken for a boy's father, who ultimately realizes that mother and child are exactly what he needs.

Laura Anthony explores the lighter side of love in *The Twenty-Four-Hour Groom*, in which a pretend marriage between a lawman and his neighbor kindles some very real feelings. WITH THESE RINGS, Patricia Thayer's Special Edition/Romance cross-line miniseries, moves into Romance with *Her Surprise Family*, with a woman who longs for a husband and home and unexpectedly finds both. And in *A Man Worth Marrying*, beloved author Phyllis Halldorson shows the touching romance between a virginal schoolteacher and a much older single dad.

Treasure this month's offerings—and keep coming back to Romance for more compelling love stories!

Enjoy,

Mary-Theresa Hussey

Mary-Theresa Hussey
Senior Editor

Please address questions and book requests to:
Silhouette Reader Service
U.S.: 3010 Walden Ave., P.O. Box 1325, Buffalo, NY 14269
Canadian: P.O. Box 609, Fort Erie, Ont. L2A 5X3

A MAN WORTH MARRYING

Phyllis Halldorson

Silhouette

R O M A N C E™

Published by Silhouette Books

America's Publisher of Contemporary Romance

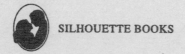

SILHOUETTE BOOKS

ISBN 0-373-19395-5

A MAN WORTH MARRYING

Visit us at www.romance.net

Printed in U.S.A.

Books by Phyllis Halldorson

Silhouette Romance

Temporary Bride #31
To Start Again #79
Mountain Melody #247
If Ever I Loved You #282
Design for Two Hearts #367
Forgotten Love #395
An Honest Lover #456
To Choose a Wife #515
Return to Raindance #566
Raindance Autumn #584
Ageless Passion, Timeless Love #653
Dream Again of Love #689
Only the Nanny Knows for Sure #760
Lady Diamond #791
More Than You Know #948
Father in the Middle #1060
Mail Order Wife #1133
A Wife for Dr. Sam #1219
The Lawman's Legacy #1255
A Man Worth Marrying #1395

Silhouette Special Edition

My Heart's Undoing #290
The Showgirl and the Professor #368
Cross My Heart #430
Ask Not of Me, Love #510
All We Know of Heaven #621
You Could Love Me #734
Luscious Lady #764
A Haven in His Arms #863
Truly Married #958
The Bride and the Baby #999
The Millionaire's Baby #1145

Silhouette Books

Silhouette Christmas Stories 1991
"A Memorable Noel"

PHYLLIS HALLDORSON

met her real-life Prince Charming at the age of sixteen. She married him a year later, and they settled down to raise a family. A compulsive reader, Phyllis dreamed of someday finding the time to write stories of her own. That time came when her two youngest children reached adolescence. When she was introduced to romance novels, she knew she had found her long-delayed vocation. After all, how could she write anything else after living all those years with her very own Silhouette hero?

Chapter One

Eve Costopoulos walked thoughtfully back to her classroom at Homestead Elementary School, after seeing to it that each of the third-grade children she tutored after school had been claimed by a parent or guardian and were on their way home.

As she approached the room, she saw a man coming out of it. A man who had no business being there, as far as she knew. There was so much vandalism at this school that the staff had been alerted to challenge any stranger they saw on campus.

He was looking down the hall in the other direction as she neared him. "Excuse me," she said, and hoped she sounded forceful. "May I help you?"

He turned quickly toward her. Even with the startled expression on his face, he was uncommonly handsome. Tall. More than six feet, but slender, with dark brown hair and blue eyes. He looked awfully familiar, but she couldn't think where she had seen him.

It only took a second for him to regain his composure.

When he did, he looked closely at her, and he must have liked what he saw. There was admiration in those wide expressive eyes. "Maybe you can," he said. "I'm looking for Ms. Evangeline Costopoulos. I understand she's a teacher here."

Now it was Eve who was startled. He was looking for her! But why? Eve taught underprivileged children in this school, which was situated in Rapid City, South Dakota, and it wasn't likely that he was the father of one of her students. He was too well dressed. For one thing, he was wearing a suit, and all the fathers she'd met so far wore jeans or cotton pants with denim jackets. Also, the suit was custom-made of fine wool. It had to be, to fit so well across his broad shoulders and still taper so exactly to his narrow waist and hips. None of the men in this area wore thousand-dollar suits.

"I'm Evangeline Costopoulos," she said. "And you are...?"

"Grayson Flint," he replied with a big smile. "I called earlier. You did get my message, didn't you?"

She blinked. "Message? What message?"

The name Grayson Flint was familiar to her, too, but she still couldn't place it.

"I called this morning and asked the school secretary if I could arrange to see you after school hours. She gave me an appointment for three o'clock. Didn't she tell you?"

Eve sighed. "I'm sorry, but we're so understaffed here that sometimes things like messages just fall through the cracks. I didn't get yours—but I'm free now. If you'd like to come into my classroom, we won't be disturbed."

She led the way back to the room and placed a worn old wooden chair in front of her desk for him, then sat down in her equally worn chair behind it. "Sorry about the uncomfortable seats, but as you probably know the school system is financially strapped. There's no room in the budget for new furniture.''

She settled back in her chair. "Now, Mr. Flint, what can I do—''

Her brain finally connected the name to the man, and she stopped short, flustered. "You're Grayson Flint, the weatherman on television!''

It came out more like an accusation than a statement, and she felt the flush of embarrassment. "I—I'm sorry. That sounded rude, and I certainly didn't mean it to. It's just that your name and your face were familiar, but I couldn't place you until just now.''

He chuckled, and she noticed he was even better looking in person than he was on TV. "Don't apologize—that happens quite often,'' he assured her. "The weather forecaster isn't the star that the news anchor is. I only have a few minutes on the air in each newscast, and the listeners are more interested in the weather patterns on the Doppler radar than they are in the meteorologist who's delivering it.''

He was not only handsome, but modest as well. That wasn't an easy combination to find.

"You're very kind,'' she said, "but I'm sure most people remember you well. Do you have a special interest in one of my students?''

"Oh no, nothing like that,'' he said. "I understand you sometimes tutor students with learning disabilities.''

That puzzled her. "Well, yes, although the children I tutor don't have disabilities so much as bad learning environments. Most of them come from impoverished homes, and don't have proper nourishment, medical care, or supervision.''

Flint looked thoughtful. "I didn't realize…" His words trailed off.

"Not only that," she continued, "but those whose parents *do* work go home to an empty house after school. The kids aren't motivated to get to school on time, or to study."

Eve knew she was getting carried away. She usually did when she talked about the deplorable conditions under which so many of the children in this district lived.

But that couldn't be this man's problem. Whether he was too modest to admit it or not, he was a television personality who made a lot of money. If he had children, they would never go hungry or without medical care.

She stopped and took a deep breath. "I'm sorry, I didn't mean to deliver a lecture. It's just that this is my first year of teaching, and I guess I'm getting my first taste of the real world. It can be pretty hard to take at times."

"That's because you're a caring and warmhearted person," he said. "And believe me, there are more like you than you think, but we'll talk about that another time. Right now I need to know if you're familiar with dyslexia."

Her eyes widened. "Dyslexia? I know that it's a reading disorder that's associated with impairment of the ability to interpret spatial relationships—"

Flint made a face and held up his hand. "Whoa there, slow down. I don't mean the textbook interpretation. I've already been given all the technical information. What I want is a translation into layman's language. What's going on in a person who has it?"

Eve wondered why he had come to her with this request. Why didn't he seek out a specialist in learning disabilities? And what was he going to do with the information? Was he gathering it for a colleague at the television station who was doing a story on it? Or did he plan to do a story himself?

Oh well, it couldn't hurt to tell him what she knew, she thought. "As I understand it, the people who suffer from dyslexia cannot grasp the meaning or sequence of letters, words or symbols, or the idea of direction. They often confuse letters or words, and may read or write words or sentences in the wrong order, such as *god* for *dog*. This causes them to have difficulty reading, and spelling."

"Have you any new information on what causes it?" he asked anxiously.

She shook her head. "Nobody knows. Sometimes there's a family history, sometimes it's due to brain damage. But generally the cause is obscure. We do know that more boys than girls have it, that dyslexic children generally have average or above-average intelligence, and that they don't differ from normal learners in their ability to hear, see and speak. Aside from that, there's really nothing else I can tell you, other than to recommend that you talk to a specialist in that field—"

"I've already done that, and I have to confess that I haven't been altogether truthful with you. Or, rather, I haven't told you everything you probably have a right to know."

She frowned, and he shifted uncomfortably in his chair. "You see, I have a daughter who's recently been diagnosed as dyslexic."

A daughter. That was one of the possibilities that hadn't occurred to Eve. Viewers don't tend to think of television personalities as family people. However, she admired his concern for his child.

"Oh, I'm so sorry," she said. "How old is she?"

Flint closed his eyes for just a moment before answering. "She's eight and in the third grade. Up until now her teachers have been reluctant to hold her back, assuming that she was just a slow starter. Now that she's finally been correctly diagnosed, she's been working with a therapist and is doing fairly well in her ability to read, but she's so far behind the other children in her grade that she desperately needs private tutoring. I'm looking for a tutor to help her catch up. I spoke to the district superintendent of schools, and he recommended you.''

"Me?'' Eve asked, surprised. ''But I don't tutor private students. I just give a little help to those in my class who show potential and a willingness to work hard in order to learn. What I do is strictly on a volunteer basis. I don't charge either the parents or the school district, but I do insist that the children attend every class, pay attention and do the light homework I assign.''

He leaned forward in his chair. ''But that's exactly what I'm asking you to do for Tinker, except I'd prefer that you work one-on-one with her—and, of course, I'll pay you. Erik Johnson says you're getting amazing results with your small group of students, and Erik's word is good enough for me.''

She felt warmed by the compliment. ''That's very nice of you to say. I gather you know our district superintendent?''

He grinned. ''Oh, yes. We in the media are on a first-name basis with most of the community leaders. It's to our mutual advantage. We give them public exposure for their pet projects, and they give us news tips. Come on, what do you say? Will you help my little girl?''

When he put it like that, it was hard to refuse him. But she really didn't have time to take on anything else. Surely someone with his money and contacts wouldn't have any trouble finding another teacher to tutor his child.

"I'm sorry, Mr. Flint—''

"Please call me Gray," he interrupted. "Grayson is too formal, and Mr. Flint is my father."

He smiled winningly, and though she knew she was being manipulated, she couldn't help being flattered. Still, she wasn't going to let him get away with it.

"All right, Gray, and I'm Eve. But much as I'd like to work with your daughter, I just can't take on anything more at this time. I'm sure there are other teachers in the area who would be willing—"

Again he interrupted. "I don't want just anyone, Eve, I want the best. Ideally that would be a teacher specially trained in reading disorders, but the only one who was available here with those credentials was let go last year because of the budget crisis. That's why I asked Erik Johnson for a recommendation, and he said there is no one better in the area than you."

"I'm flattered, truly I am," she said, "but—"

"He also told me you tutored one of his children who has dyslexia, and that that child is now making straight As in high school."

She sighed. "That's true, but that was when I was still in college, and a lot of it was just dumb luck."

"Not according to Erik. His praise for your skill as a teacher is boundless. He tells me you've even discussed the possibility of going back to school and getting credentials in teaching special education."

She wished Mr. Johnson wouldn't be so vocal in his praise of her. It's true that his young son had been an especially difficult case, and that after several starts and stops she'd finally managed to capture his attention and turn him on to learning. Unfortunately, his father's gratitude knew no bounds, and sometimes put her in an awkward position, like this one.

"I would like to get into the field of special education,

yes, but right now I can't do justice to the youngsters I'm already responsible for if I take on more. My regular class is so overcrowded that it's not possible for me to give the students as much of my time as they need, so I choose the ones I feel are most likely to learn with a little extra help. I tutor them for half an hour after school on Mondays through Thursdays. That doesn't leave me much time for anything else.''

She tapped her pencil on her desktop. ''I don't mean to get personal, Gray, but I have no doubt that you can afford a tutor for your child. The parents of my students can't. If I don't give them extra time and help, it's unlikely they'll ever catch up and be productive citizens—even though the potential is there.''

He frowned. ''Of course I can afford to pay a tutor, and I'm prepared to pay you whatever you feel is fair. It's not the expense I'm concerned about, it's the quality of the help she'll be getting. She tries so hard, but learning is difficult for her and it's affecting her self-esteem. She's at the awkward stage, anyway, and being so far behind her classmates in school just adds to her burdens.''

Eve's heart melted. He was right—his youngster could be permanently damaged emotionally if she didn't receive expert help soon. But what could she do? She was no expert on dyslexia. Gray probably knew more about it than she did. He'd been dealing with it—albeit unknowingly—for all of his daughter's life. Plus, Eve could only stretch her time and energy so far.

''I have no right to put my little girl's problems on your shoulders. It's just that I'm so worried about her. Her mother and I have handled this wrong right from the beginning. Except for the fact that her speech was difficult to understand, Tinker was always bright and cheerful before she started school. But that all changed once she got in first grade. We realized that some of her antics we'd thought were deliberate were actually the result of clumsiness, and she didn't seem to know her right hand from her left. Her grades got steadily worse, and we thought she was just not paying attention. We tried to help her but she was so easily distracted and frustrated—''

"Those are classic signs of dyslexia," Eve interrupted, "but they could also signal other problems. Believe me, you're not alone in this. Actually, you were lucky to have caught on so quickly. Some dyslexic children aren't diagnosed until they're in middle or even high school."

Gray had his back to her, so she couldn't see his expression, but she saw him nod his head. "We know that now, but at the time we scolded her, even punished her—''

His voice broke, and Eve had to use all her self-control to stay where she was and not get up and go over to him. She was here to teach the children, not to comfort their fathers, but with this father it was hard to remember that!

She cleared her throat. "That's a natural reaction. After all, you had no way of knowing she wasn't just goofing off. Please, don't blame yourself. These things happen, and it's not anybody's fault.

"By the way, I don't think I caught her name correctly. It sounded as if you were calling her Tinker."

This time he turned to face her before answering. "No, you didn't hear wrong. Her mother is the free-spirited type, and she wanted to name the baby Tinkerbell after the character in Peter Pan, but I wouldn't allow it. Who ever heard of a Tinkerbell growing up to be CEO of a company, or president of the United States?"

Eve chuckled. "I see you have grand ambitions for your daughter."

A ghost of a smile hovered at the corners of his mouth.

"Don't all parents? But truly, all I want for her is to be happy, and giving her a name like that would only subject her to ridicule. I insisted we name her Sarah, but her mother didn't like that and started calling her Tinker. It stuck."

Eve sensed a family squabble of serious proportions over the naming of the child, and knew she should not probe, but she was curious.

"By which name does your daughter prefer to be called?" she asked.

"Oh, everyone calls her Tinker now. Even me," he admitted. "She hardly remembers she has another name. I stopped calling her Sarah when she was younger—I realized it just confused her."

His gaze roamed over Eve. "While we're on the subject of names, are you by any chance related to Alexander Costopoulos, the building contractor?"

"He's my father," Eve told him. "Do you know him?"

"Sure do. He added a couple of rooms to the television station last year. How is Alex? I seem to remember hearing he'd fallen at one of the construction sites and broken some bones."

"A couple in his right leg, yes," she confirmed. "The doctor assures us they're healing nicely, but Dad hates not being able to get around without the help of crutches or a walker."

"I'll bet he does," Gray agreed. "He doesn't like to be slowed down. Be sure and give him my best."

"I certainly will," she said. "But now to get back to the subject of your daughter. I'm truly sorry, but I'm over-extended as it is—"

"Why don't you meet her before you make up your mind," he cut in. "That seems only fair. Then, if you still feel you can't work her in, I'll accept it and try to find someone else.''

Eve sighed. ''Don't think for a minute I don't know what you're doing, Gray Flint. You're playing on my weakness for children. You think that if I see what a sweet, intelligent and deserving child she is, I'll reconsider.''

He looked her straight in the eye. ''Damn right. Can you tell me you wouldn't do the same thing if our positions were reversed?''

She thought for a moment. Gray was a father desperate to find help for his daughter, and she admired him for that—enough that she wasn't going to lie to him. ''No, I can't, but our positions aren't reversed, and if I wear myself out, I'm not going to be good for *any* of my students.''

''Okay, I can appreciate that,'' he admitted. ''I sure don't want you to endanger your health. But there's only a week of school left. If you could work Tinker into your busy schedule now, I'll hire you to work for a couple of hours every weekday all summer.''

Gray looked around the room, and Eve was sure he was seeing it for the first time. Until now, his only concern had been to convince her to tutor his daughter.

''This is a pretty depressing place to work, isn't it,'' he observed. ''Why don't you transfer to another school?''

She wondered if he realized how callous that sounded to her, although she was sure he hadn't meant it that way.

Rising from her chair, she went to stand by him. ''And if I did, who would teach the students here?''

He blinked. ''Well I—there must be teachers who are looking for jobs.''

''There are, but none of them want to work here. Would

you?'' She looked at him. "What school does Tinker go to?"

He appeared disconcerted. "She goes to a private school, but—"

"Does her building have a leaky roof?" she interrupted.

"No—"

"Is the paint peeling off its walls, both inside and out?"

"No, but—"

"Is the heating system in constant need of repair?"

His tone rose with frustration. "No. Damn it all, Eve—"

"Of course it doesn't have those problems," she pointed out, "because its affluent parents and alumni can afford to keep it in good condition. Also, they can raise the tuition anytime it's necessary to pay for the best teachers, so they draw from the top applicants."

Gray finally found an opening into the conversation. "From all I've heard, you're a good teacher. So why aren't you working at a school like Tinker's?"

She was ready for him. "You're right, I am a good teacher. In fact I'm an excellent teacher. I studied hard in college and learned my lessons well, plus I care about my students. I want to see them learn, but I also want the ones who are capable of it to excel. With all they have working against them, that will never happen if they can't get dedicated instructors to teach them."

"Now surely you're not the only 'dedicated instructor' in the whole area," Gray taunted lightly.

"No, I'm not," she admitted, refusing to acknowledge his teasing. "But it's easier for me to be noble. I don't have children of my own to teach and raise, or a husband who needs me to share time with him, too."

He eyed her left hand. "You're not married, then?"

She shook her head. "No, but that doesn't mean I don't need time off from my work. Some of these children will break your heart if you let them."

"And you let them," he said softly as his gentle blue eyes searched hers.

To her dismay, her heart speeded up at his tone, and she felt all fuzzy and warm. She fought the urge to let herself be drawn closer.

Watch it, girl. This guy's way out of your league. And more important, he's married!

She stepped back and turned away from him. "I'm sorry but I have to get home. I have papers to grade and a school board meeting to attend tonight. If we can't get the board to put a new roof on this building this summer, we're going to be sloshing around in water ankle-deep by next fall. At the rate donations are coming in for the roofing fund, it's going to be years instead of a month before we collect enough."

Gray gazed thoughtfully at Eve. "I have an idea. I'll make a hefty donation to the school's roofing fund, in addition to paying your salary, if you agree to tutor Tinker."

Eve gasped, unable to believe what she'd heard. "Are you trying to bribe me?" she asked tentatively.

"That, I am," he admitted with a twinkle in his eyes.

Eve laughed. She couldn't resist Gray's winning ways—or his offer. In addition, it was an honor to be recommended to him as highly as she had been by the district superintendent. "All right," she reluctantly agreed. "I'll consider tutoring Tinker. But I think I should meet her first to establish trust before the tutoring begins. When do you want this meeting to take place?"

He glanced at his watch. "How about this time tomorrow? I can bring her here, but I'd really prefer that you come to my house. Since that's where you would be tutoring her, I'd like you to get acquainted with it, too."

"Tomorrow at this time and at your house will be fine," she said, striving for a tone of brisk efficiency, "if you'll just give me your address and phone number. Oh, and I assume your wife will be there, too?"

He looked momentarily uncomprehending, but recovered quickly. "I don't have a wife," he said. "Tinker's mother and I are divorced."

Chapter Two

Gray saw the surprise in Eve's expression, and only then realized that he hadn't told her he was a single father. "I'm sorry," he apologized. "I didn't intend to mislead you. Tinker's mother and I have been divorced for three years. We share custody, but she works part-time as hostess at a restaurant, and because of our rather unconventional working hours—I go to work very early in the morning and she works four hours, midafternoon and early evening—I have Tinker from the time she gets home from school until bedtime. Bambi has her throughout the night and until she goes off to school in the morning. We alternate weekends."

Now Eve looked confused, and he braced himself for further questions. He didn't like discussing his private business with others, but he would make an exception in her case if she pressed the issue.

She didn't. "I see," she said instead. "Then I'll meet with you and Tinker tomorrow."

They started walking toward the door, then Eve suddenly stopped and turned to face him. "One more thing," she said seriously. "Does Tinker know you're arranging to have her tutored during school vacation?"

He shook his head. "Not yet. She's not going to be pleased, and I wanted to be sure I could find an available teacher before I told her. I didn't want to upset her unnecessarily."

Eve looked perplexed. "But isn't that what you'll be doing by introducing her to me? It's not at all likely that I'll accept the position—"

He didn't like the sound of that, but decided to play it lightly. Touching the tip of her slender nose, he smiled. "Ah-ah, there you go again—making up your mind before you've explored all the facts."

She frowned, and he decided he'd better not press his luck. Reluctantly he withdrew his hand before he could give in to the overpowering urge to run his fingers through her glistening black curls.

"I'll talk to her tonight, explain to her why it's necessary, and tell her I've arranged for a teacher to come by tomorrow afternoon to meet her. Everything will be all right. You'll see," he assured her.

He gave her his address and phone number, then thanked her for taking the time to talk to him and left the school building.

As he drove, his mind shifted back to Eve Costopoulos. She wasn't at all what he'd expected. She was much younger, for one thing. Erik, the district superintendent, hadn't mentioned her age, and for some reason he'd pictured someone closer to his own. This one seemed hardly out of her teens—although she had to be in her early twenties, at least, in order to have graduated from college and taught for close to a year.

He also hadn't expected her to be such a knockout!

Taller than average, possibly five foot eight, with ample curves that couldn't be downplayed even by the simple gray skirt and matching cardigan sweater she wore with a tailored white blouse.

She had ebony hair that was a twirling mass of curls swirling around her shoulders making her look like a gypsy, and he'd been disconcerted at his strong urge to tangle his fingers in it.

He stopped for a stop sign, but his contemplation didn't even slow down as he started up again and made a left turn.

As for Eve's eyes, it was best not to think of them at all. They were black as her hair, and every bit as unsettling, with their deep-set beauty and their way of looking straight into him. They stirred up feelings that he didn't welcome, called up emotions he'd sworn never to let get the better of him again.

So why was he so eager to have her tutor his daughter? If his initial attraction to her was this keen, then having her in his house, working with his child several days a week, could be disastrous!

He swore softly. What had gotten into him? Once he'd finally taken all he could of Bambi's capriciousness and asked for a divorce, he'd vowed never to get seriously involved with a woman again. He sure had no intention of falling in love!

He knew there were adequate teachers who would be happy to have part-time employment for the summer. They might not come as highly recommended as Eve, but they could have done the job. Why hadn't he just accepted her refusal and let it go at that—?

Because he was spoiled, that's why. As a minor celebrity in this small city, he was used to getting his own way.

And he wasn't prepared to have a slip of a girl tell him he couldn't beg, borrow or buy her expert services—

The car in front of him stopped suddenly, and he slammed on his brake and almost rear-ended it. He'd been so lost in his musing that he hadn't seen the red light ahead.

Enough of this old nonsense! He wasn't going to take a chance on getting involved with any woman, and certainly not one who was his daughter's teacher. He didn't have Eve's home phone number, but he could call her at school in the morning and tell her that he was regretfully willing to accept her initial refusal, after all. He knew she'd be relieved.

Now that that was settled, maybe he could concentrate on his driving, on picking up Tinker from Judy, the baby-sitter who was a stay-at-home mom and who was on call when his work hours collided with his custody responsibility—without wrecking his sports car.

Gray rolled out of bed at three o'clock the next morning when the alarm went off. He had to get up early every morning in order to be ready to do the weather at five, on the first newscast of the day. It wasn't much of a hardship. He usually retired at nine on weeknights, and got by nicely on six hours of sleep.

His first thought was of Eve and his need to call her, but obviously it was much too early. She wouldn't be at school for at least four more hours.

Unfortunately things hadn't gone last night as he'd planned. In fact, everything that could go wrong had. The outcome was that he hadn't even seen his daughter, let alone been able to talk to her about being tutored.

He sighed. Not that it really mattered, since he wasn't going to hire Eve anyway.

But by then it was too late to phone her. After all the fuss he'd made yesterday about wanting her, and only her, to tutor his child, it would be impolite to wait until the last minute to contact her and tell her he'd changed his mind. No, now he'd just wait until she arrived and then graciously accept her initial refusal to take the job.

A suspicion niggled at him, but he shook it off. He wasn't having second thoughts about not hiring her. Certainly not! He hadn't deliberately frittered away the time—it had just gotten away from him, was all.

He had no intention of pursuing any kind of relationship with her. Not even a business one.

Eve drove through the neighborhood of well-kept upscale homes. The houses were large, but not ostentatious. Although the lawns were still brown and the big old trees just beginning to leaf, she could see that they received good care during the warmer seasons.

She spotted the address she was looking for, and pulled over to the curb in front of the house. It was one of the smaller homes on the block: a one-story Tudor-style built of red brick with a red tile roof. Handsome as well as sturdy.

Getting out of her silver-gray compact, she approached the house and climbed the steps to the covered porch. She rang the bell, but as she waited she was sorely tempted to turn and run. Although she'd promised to consider tutoring Gray's daughter, she didn't like being outwitted, especially by a man who attracted her so strongly. She neither needed nor wanted a man in her life at this time. Certainly not one who had already been married and had an eight-year-old child!

Before she could act on her urge to flee, the inside door opened. Gray stood on the other side of the storm door;

he must have been watching for her, to have gotten there so quickly.

"Hi," he said, and unlocked the outside door to open it. "I...I hope you haven't been too badly inconvenienced by my insistence that you come here instead of meeting at school."

Eve was struck by the fact that he seemed ill at ease today. He hadn't been at all unsure of himself yesterday.

"It's out of my way, but not much," she said as she walked into the foyer and looked around. The living room was on the right, the dining room on the left and separated from the kitchen behind it by a chest-high breakfast bar. Straight ahead was a long hall with rooms on either side and at the end. The floors were covered in thick brown-and-beige carpeting, and the furniture was heavy and masculine. Expensive but serviceable.

"You have a very attractive home," she said. "Did you decorate it yourself?"

He smiled. "Not exactly. When I moved in, I hired a decorator to work with me. And then Bambi got into the act—"

"Is Bambi your ex-wife's name?" she interrupted. "Or am I misunderstanding again?"

He sighed. "No, you're not misunderstanding. I told you she was flighty, but you really have to know her to know what I mean. She was christened Bernice after her grandmother, but she didn't like that name, so she started calling herself Bambi after she saw the Disney movie when she was a child. Now she even uses it as her legal name."

"My word." Eve murmured. "She certainly is creative." It was the only way she could think of to describe the muddled impression she was getting of his ex-wife.

"Oh yes, she is that," he agreed as he helped her off

with her coat. His strong hand touched her shoulder, totally by accident she was sure, but it sent a tingle down her spine.

"I have fresh coffee made," he said as he hung the coat in the closet of the small entryway. "If you'd like to go sit down in the living room, I'll bring the cups and things out."

She'd smelled the coffee perking the minute she stepped inside the house, and she wasn't going to be coy about accepting a cup. She needed something to keep her wide awake and shrewd enough to deal with this man.

"Let me help," she said, and followed him into the kitchen. There she saw a carafe, china cups, saucers, sugar, creamer and silver spoons arranged on a tray. She was sure this wasn't the way he had his coffee when he was alone. He'd gone to some trouble to make things nice for her.

He accepted her offer without hesitation. "If you really want to, you can bring the can of soda and the glass of ice over there on the counter. That's for Tinker."

She picked up the items and walked into the living room, where Gray set the tray down on the coffee table in front of the sofa that faced the brick fireplace.

"I'd intended to light a fire," he said, motioning for her to sit down, "but I had some errands to run after I picked Tinker up at school, and by the time we got home, it was too late."

She had the distinct impression that he was grasping for small talk rather than coming to grips with the issue that had brought her here—but why?

"Everything is just right," she assured him as she settled herself on the couch. "But you shouldn't have gone to so much trouble. Where is Tinker, by the way?"

Gray sat down beside Eve. "She's watching television

in my office down the hall. She doesn't have many friends. Once in a while she'll bring a classmate home with her, or she'll be invited to go to someone else's house, but mostly she keeps to herself. I think it's her poor grades. She doesn't want to talk about them with the other students, so she remains aloof.''

Eve felt a stab of compassion. "Oh, the poor child," she murmured. "She really does need help. That type of thing can damage her self-image for a lifetime.''

"I'm well aware of that," Gray said. "But there's something I have to tell you before we go any further with this.''

He shifted nervously on the cushion. "I didn't get a chance to talk to Tinker last evening about having her tutored.''

Eve's eyes widened with dismay. "But you promised—''

"I know," he said mournfully, "and I had every intention of doing it, but when I left the school after talking with you I got a call on my cell phone from the TV station, telling me some new weather-tracking equipment we'd ordered had been delivered. I needed to be there to learn how it's set up, and how to use it.''

He shrugged. "All I could do was phone Bambi and tell her to pick Tinker up at the baby-sitter's instead of at my house. I hadn't seen her since I left you yesterday afternoon until she came home from school today. By then it was so late that I decided I'd better wait and talk it over with you. You know better how to handle children than I do.''

"She doesn't know why I'm here." Eve's voice was filled with chagrin. She felt trapped. This was supposed to be a getting-to-know-each-other meeting to see if she and Tinker could connect as student and teacher. It was important that the child accept being tutored before her father sprang his choice of tutor on her. This wasn't fair to either student or teacher.

Gray ran his fingers through his hair. "No, she doesn't," he admitted. "I'm sorry, Eve, but it's just one of those things that snowballed out of my control. I didn't even have a chance to call you and postpone the meeting. As long as you're here now, though, I would like you to meet her. She knows you're coming."

Eve glared at him. "You told her about me?"

He sighed. "I had to. She saw me fixing the coffee things, and asked who was coming." The corners of his mouth raised in a small smile. "I don't usually use the best china and silver when I serve coffee to neighbors or the gang I work with."

Eve had to admit that sounded reasonable. "What did you tell her about me?"

"Only that we had some business to discuss," he assured her. "She didn't think anything of it. In my profession you meet a lot of new people, so she's used to strangers coming and going."

Eve fidgeted with her purse. "I really don't see any advantage to meeting her until you've told her about the tutoring sessions." She hemmed.

She was surprised to discover that she'd actually been looking forward to seeing Gray's little girl. Eve was curious about how the youngster looked, how she was progressing with her schoolwork, and how she and Gray got along together.

"Please, Eve, stay for just a little while. I always introduce Tinker to my guests. She expects it, and if you run off without even saying hello to her, it's going to hurt her feelings."

Gray caught himself up short. What was the matter with

him anyway? He'd wanted a graceful reason not to hire her. Now here it was, handed to him on the proverbial silver platter, and he was practically pleading with her to stay and get acquainted!

Meanwhile, Eve could see it was important that she stay at least long enough to meet Tinker and have a cup of coffee. She relaxed and leaned back against the leather upholstery. "All right, if you really think it's best, I'd love to meet her. But make it plain that I'm just a business associate."

"I'm sorry it has to be that way," he said sadly, "but I understand."

He stood up and headed for the hall. "Now, if you'd like to pour us some coffee I'll go get Tinker."

Gray returned in a few minutes with a young girl in tow. She was wearing a black skort and white cotton blouse: the private school uniform. And she showed promise of blooming into an attractive teenager in a few years, but for now she was all arms and legs—bigger than most children her age and lacking the gracefulness of a smaller child.

Eve felt a twinge of empathy. She'd been too big and awkward at that age, also. She didn't know what Bambi looked like, but she could see a lot of Gray in his daughter. The girl had his dark brown hair and blue eyes.

"Tinker, I'd like you to meet Ms. Costopoulos," Gray said.

He turned to Eve. "And Eve, this is my daughter, Sarah, but everybody calls her Tinker."

The child hung back and looked at the floor shyly, so Eve took the initiative. "I'm very pleased to meet you," she said softly. "May I call you Tinker?"

"I...I guess so," Tinker said unenthusiastically, still not looking up.

"Fine," Eve answered, keeping her tone friendly. "My name is Evangeline, but everyone calls me Eve. I hope you will too."

Tinker didn't respond, but for the first time she raised her head and looked up at Eve. There was a strong negative emotion in her eyes. Fear? Resentment? Eve couldn't tell.

"Are you going to be my teacher?" Tinker asked angrily.

That stunned Eve. What was going on here? Gray had just told her that Tinker didn't know he was making plans to have her tutored!

Her head jerked up to scan Gray's face, but he looked as shocked as she was. He scowled and shook his head, then hunkered down beside Tinker and put his arm around her. "Honey, Ms. Costopoulos—Eve—is a teacher, but she teaches third grade at a school on the other side of town. Who told you she was going to be your teacher?"

Tinker looked at him. "Mom did. She said I'd have to study all summer because you were going to get a teacher to—to come to the house and make sure I did."

Her face contorted and there was a sob in her voice. "Please, Daddy, don't make me do that. I do study. Honest I do, but it's so hard. I'll never learn all that stuff."

Gray muttered an oath under his breath as he drew his daughter closer. Bambi! If he didn't know better he'd think she was deliberately sabotaging his efforts to bring Tinker up to the learning level of the rest of her class.

Unfortunately, it wasn't that simple. Bambi didn't mean any harm; she just didn't understand how important it was to tread softly so as not to further damage Tinker's already low self-esteem. He should have known better than to tell her what he was planing to do until it was an accomplished fact.

"Tinker," he said gently, "I'm afraid your mom misunderstood. What I want to do is find a teacher who will come here for just a couple of hours several afternoons a week, and help you catch up with the rest of your class. She won't push you, but she'll teach you all you've missed because of your dyslexia. When school starts again next fall, you'll be able to read, write, and do the arithmetic along with the others."

Tinker scrutinized Eve, and there was fear in her eyes. "No, I don't want her to teach me," she cried, and threw her arms around Gray's neck.

Eve was getting more distressed by the minute. Tinker didn't want to be tutored, but she clearly needed the one-on-one help.

Eve spoke before Gray had a chance. "Tinker, you don't need to be afraid of me. Your father thought you and I should get acquainted because I can help you—but only if you want my help."

She glanced around and picked up the glass of cola and ice she'd poured for Tinker. "Here, honey," she said, and held it out to the youngster. "Your dad said this glass of soda is for you."

Tinker hesitated, then raised her head and looked back at Eve. After a moment, she twisted out of her father's arms and walked across the floor to take the beverage.

"Why don't you sit beside me here on the couch," Eve said, making it a suggestion, not a command.

Tinker said nothing, but finally did sit down.

Next, Eve deliberately shifted her attention from Tinker to Gray, giving Tinker a chance to observe her. "How do you take your coffee, Gray? Cream and sugar?"

"Black," Gray said, and stood to walk over and get the cup and saucer.

He pulled up an upholstered occasional chair and sat down next to his daughter.

For a few minutes there was strained silence, then Gray spoke. "Tinker, I bought cookies at the bakery and put them in the cookie jar, then forgot to bring them out. Would you mind getting them?"

The child's eyes lit up. "Peanut butter with chocolate chips?" she asked.

Gray nodded. "Your favorite."

"All right!" she said excitedly as she jumped up and headed for the kitchen.

Gray let out his breath. "Now where do we go from here?" he asked anxiously.

"Nowhere," Eve said firmly. "It's out of the question for me to tutor Tinker now. We got off to an impossible start, and she'll never trust me. I'm sorry to say this, but the first thing you must do is *undo* the damage her mother has done. Then you'll have to find another tutor."

His cup clattered in the saucer as he put it down on the low table. "Unfortunately, I made the mistake of discussing my plans with Bambi." There was bitterness in his tone.

"Did you tell your wife you didn't want Tinker to know you were making plans to have her privately tutored?" Eve asked.

Gray ran his hand over his face. "Ex-wife," he corrected her. "And of course I did, but when did that ever stop her. She gets upset if I make plans for Tinker without telling her, but when I do tell her, she broadcasts it all over town. If the kids at school hear Tinker's being tutored, they'll undoubtedly tease her, call her dumb or stupid. Children can be so cruel without ever meaning to."

Eve knew all about that, both from her experience as a child when she'd been teased about her long, Greek, almost-unpronounceable last name, as well as her height, and now as a teacher whose pupils constantly fought for recognition and didn't care how they got it. They often taunted those who were different, or spread vicious rumors about a student who was smarter or had a few more possessions than most of the others did.

She shuddered. "Yes, I know," she murmured softly, wishing there was a way she could shoulder some of his child's pain.

Tinker's young voice came from the kitchen. "Daddy, I can't find the cookie jar. I think it's on the top shelf, but I can't reach it."

Gray jumped out of the chair. "Just stay where you are, and I'll get it," he called as he hurried into the other room. "I don't want you to climb up on something and fall."

They were back in a few seconds with a plate of cookies that Gray passed around. Tinker took two, then picked up her glass of soda. "I'm going back to the office and watch television," she announced sharply, and turned to walk away.

"Just a minute, young lady," Gray said in a tone that stopped his daughter in her tracks. "I didn't hear you ask to be excused."

"Please-may-I-be-excused." She ran all the words together, her back still turned to them.

"Not until you ask politely," Gray reprimanded, and it was clear that it embarrassed him to have to discipline his daughter in front of a third person. Being caught in the middle of it embarrassed Eve, too, but she admired him for not letting Tinker get away with being disrespectful.

"Oh, Daddy," she said mutinously, but she turned to face them, and once more asked—politely this time—to be excused.

Gray looked relieved. "Yes, you may," he answered crisply. Tinker turned around and headed for the back of the house.

When they heard a door slam shut, Gray sighed and dropped down on the couch beside Eve. "I don't know what to say, how to apologize for my daughter's behavior." He sounded more concerned than humiliated. "I know you'll find it hard to believe, but she's usually too meek rather than too aggressive."

Eve wished she could touch him in a reassuring gesture, but knew that would be a big mistake. There was too much magnetism between them. Neither of them had admitted it, but it had been building since their chance encounter in the hallway of her school the previous afternoon.

That sort of thing had never happened to her before. The attraction she'd felt for men had usually taken time to build, and had never really gone anywhere. Except with Damian, and she wasn't going to think about him....

"I'm not a bit surprised or offended by Tinker's behavior, Gray," she told him. "The poor child is terrified."

He looked at her and blinked. "What do you mean, 'terrified'?"

"She's afraid of trying something new and failing again," Eve said gently. "Apparently her mother isn't very supportive of the idea of having her tutored, and let Tinker know it. Then you sprang me on her—"

"I admit that was a mistake. I should have listened to you. You warned me—"

"But you couldn't have known your ex-wife would be so...so..." How could she put it without criticizing?

"I think *insensitive* is the word you're looking for," he said harshly. "But I should have known. I lived with her for eight years..." His voice trailed off.

Eve wondered what he meant by that, but she wasn't going to prolong this conversation. She took a sip of her now-cold coffee, then put the cup down and stood.

"I'm truly sorry this happened," she said. "It will make the process of having Tinker tutored much more difficult. But I urge you to keep trying to find someone she likes and trusts. Have you tried counseling? That might help."

Gray stood also. He didn't answer her question, but posed one of his own. "Eve, are you sure you can't work with her? I'll have her counseled if that's what you suggest. You and the counselor could work together, but I have a gut feeling that you can handle my daughter better than anyone else."

Eve shook her head sadly. "You don't even know me, Gray, and I don't know Tinker. I'm sure, though, that any help I could have given her has been spoiled by her mother's interference. Both Tinker and your ex-wife would resent me if I tried, and it would only harm Tinker further."

Eve picked up her purse and headed for the door. "May I have my coat, please."

"Are you sure there's nothing I can say to change your mind?" He was surprised to hear himself ask the question as he followed her to the closet by the door and took out her coat. The object wasn't to change her mind, dammit, it was to agree with her that the situation was hopeless.

She shook her head. "No, but I really am sorry."

She shrugged into the coat Gray was holding for her, then turned to face him. "It's been nice meeting you, Gray," she said, and stuck out her hand. "Tinker too. I wish you the very best of luck with a different tutor."

Gray took her hand and cradled it in both of his. His were warm and strong, and there was a tingle of electricity that flowed from them into hers. He felt it, too. She could see it in his eyes. The blue of his pupils darkened and softened.

"You haven't seen the last of me, Ms. Evangeline Costopoulos," he murmured as he squeezed her hand and released it.

She turned and, not even sure why, she fled.

Chapter Three

The weekend came and went, and Monday morning was sunny and bright. But the nape of Eve's neck tingled, so she wasn't surprised when storm clouds began gathering by noon. Ever since she was a little girl, she'd been forecasting the weather by paying attention to a tightening at her nape. But she no longer bothered to mention it. Nobody believed her.

By the time she was ready to dismiss her class, the skies had opened up and were pouring rain onto the roof, which in turn dripped water through the ceiling and noisily into buckets strategically placed by teachers and students in hope of keeping themselves and their school supplies dry.

It was maddening, and Eve clenched her jaws in frustration. The fund that had been started for a new roof was increasing, but much too slowly. If only there was something she could do! Eve thought. But on her salary she could only make token contributions. If she'd accepted the summer job Gray Flint had offered her, he would have donated money to the roofing fund....

Tinker. Eve tried not to think about the child, because that led to thoughts of Gray, and she didn't want to reflect on him. She'd been right when she refused to go ahead and tutor Tinker in spite of the child's objections. A student had to be willing in order to learn.

Eve was just getting ready to dismiss the children when Jessica, the school secretary, came into the room, positively glowing with excitement.

"Eve, you have a phone call," she said. "It's Gray Flint. He says he has to speak to you, that it's urgent. You never told me you knew him!"

Jess was the consummate hero-worshiper, and anyone in the public eye was hero material for her. Eve couldn't help grinning, even as her own stomach filled with fluttering butterflies and tickles rippled up and down her spine. Gray projected her into orbit, too, but it wasn't hero worship. It was a much more perilous attraction than that.

"Thank you, Jess," she said without satisfying the other woman's curiosity. "Will you keep an eye on the kids? I won't be but a minute."

Without waiting for an answer, she left the room and headed for the office. Why was Gray calling her? After all, they'd agreed that she couldn't tutor Tinker. Last time they saw each other, he'd sort of indicated he might be in touch with her again, but that was four days ago. Besides, she hadn't actually believed he meant it.

She walked into the outer office and picked up the telephone. "Gray, this is Eve Costopoulos."

"Eve," he said, and sounded relieved. "I'm sorry to bother you at school, but I neglected to get your home phone number."

"That's okay," she replied. "Is something wrong?"

"No. Actually something's very right. Tinker has agreed to be tutored, and she wants you to do it."

"Oh?" Eve said skeptically. That sounded somewhat suspicious given the way the youngster had objected when first approached about it. "Are you sure you didn't coerce her into it—?"

"I swear, I didn't put any pressure on her," he interrupted. "Bambi and I just explained to her why it was so important that she have help in catching up with the rest of her classmates."

Eve's stomach muscles knotted. "You and Bambi?" Her tone betrayed her uncertainty. "And how did you get her approval?"

He chuckled. "I don't blame you for being skeptical. I admit Bambi's pretty scatterbrained, but she does want what's best for her daughter. Once I went over the situation with her, she understood why it was necessary—and helped me convince Tinker."

"Well, I think that's great," she assured him. "I know several teachers who are looking for summer employment. If you like, I can give you their names—"

"No. Wait," he interrupted. "Didn't you hear me? Tinker wants *you* to tutor her. I didn't even mention you. It was her own request. She asked for you."

Eve felt her eyes widen. "Really?"

"Really," Gray assured her. "Look, we don't have time to discuss this now—I know you have to get back to your students. I'm calling to ask if you'll have dinner with me tonight. We can work out the details then. I have a baby-sitter I can call."

Common sense told Eve that she should say no to a social engagement disguised as a business meeting, but then, when had she let common sense stand in the way of something she wanted to do as much as she wanted to go to dinner with Gray? After all, she wasn't his daughter's teacher—yet.

"I'd like that," she admitted. "I usually get home by three-thirty."

"Good," he said, and he really sounded pleased. "Okay if I pick you up around six-thirty?"

"Fine," she agreed. "If you have a piece of paper and a pencil handy, I'll give you my address and phone number."

Eve was bathed, dressed and ready to go early, so she used the extra time to straighten up her already immaculate apartment. It consisted of a living room, kitchen/dining area, bedroom and bath in one of the city's newer apartment complexes. This one had been built by her dad's construction company.

She heard the doorbell ring, and a wave of warmth swept over her. That would be Gray! She hurried to the door, and a glance through the peephole revealed him standing on the other side. Quickly she unlatched the locks and opened the door.

For a moment they just stood there looking at each other. Gray was wearing a dark blue suit, and looked suave as always. She was glad she'd selected her above-the-knee burnt-orange long-sleeve chemise—very plain but elegant. With the addition of a glowing amber necklace and earrings, she could go anywhere and be appropriately dressed.

She finally broke the spell. "Please, come in Gray."

There was no foyer; the door opened right into the living room. She stepped back to let him enter. As he walked past, she caught a faint whiff of his expensive shaving lotion. It was heady stuff: understated, but enticing.

She closed the door, and Gray's gaze roamed over her. "You look lovely," he said huskily.

"Thank you," she replied, at a loss for words to ex-press how much his admiration meant to her. "How...how much time do we have? Can we sit down and talk for a while or..."

He shook his head. "I'm afraid not. I made reservations for seven, and the restaurant is clear across town."

"Oh, then I'll get my purse," she said.

Outside, he led her to a bright red Jaguar and helped her in.

"What a beautiful car!" she exclaimed. "It looks new."

He beamed as he climbed in behind the steering wheel. "It is. It's my one extravagance."

"What a joy it must be to drive," she said. "My poor old buggy is ten years old and badly in need of a paint job—but I'm not complaining, it runs well."

He glanced at her as he started the engine and pulled away from the curb. "You're going to have to convince me that you've been driving for ten years. You don't look old enough."

She smiled. Even when using a cliché, he sounded sincere. "Ten years ago, I wasn't even old enough to get my learner's permit. Dad and Mom gave me the car secondhand when I graduated from City College. I had enrolled at the University at Brookings to get my BA, and needed something to get around in."

She thought she saw him wince. "I feel like I'm robbing the cradle. I'm thirty-six," he admitted.

She couldn't help but laugh. "Lighten up, grandpa," she teased. "It's not as if you were taking me out to propose marriage. This is just a business dinner, remember?"

"I'll try my best not to forget," he muttered so low that she wasn't sure she'd heard right.

The restaurant Gray had chosen was the newest and the

nicest one in town. The walls were paneled in wood, the lights were dim, and the diners were seated in secluded booths with shimmering votive candles in stained glass holders on the tables.

"Oh, it's lovely," Eve breathed as the hostess seated them and handed them each a large menu.

"You haven't been here before?" Gray asked.

"No, I haven't," she admitted. "I'm afraid it's out of my price range, but I read the food critic's review when it opened."

"The menu is pretty much all American, but their chef is a master at cooking it." He opened his menu. "They're already known for their prime rib, and with good reason. I highly recommend it, but don't hesitate to order anything that appeals to you."

The cocktail waitress came, and Eve asked for white wine; Gray ordered Scotch on the rocks. When the woman had gone, he closed his menu and laid it aside. "So, are you glad there's only one more week of school?"

She looked over the top of her menu. "I'm positively ecstatic," she said with a sigh.

Before Gray could answer the cocktail waitress returned with their drinks, and almost immediately after that their server came to take their order. Eve followed Gray's lead and asked for the prime rib, but the petite cut.

When they'd settled on the choice of side dishes and soups, the server left, and Eve took a sip of her wine. It was good, and she sighed and leaned back against the thick brown leather upholstery of the booth. "Now, what was it you wanted to talk to me about? You did say Tinker has agreed to be tutored, didn't you?"

He grinned. "Yes, I did, and I don't think Bambi will give me any more trouble about it. She's not malicious. I've also talked with Tinker, explained just what would be expected of her by a tutor and how much easier school will be for her once she's caught up with the rest of her class. I let her make the decision, and she decided she wants to do it after all.''

Eve breathed a sigh of relief. She was glad Tinker was no longer afraid of her. Whether deliberately or not, Bambi had frightened the child with a variation on the "wicked witch" theme.

Eve was beginning to wonder about this woman. What kind of mother would frighten her own daughter into not wanting to go to school?

Eve knew the answer. It was the same type who frightened her children into behaving by threatening them with the police. Eve had met parents like her before, but she hadn't expected to find one in a family like the Flints.

She was so absorbed in her thoughts that she jumped when Gray spoke again. "Eve? What's the matter? You haven't ruled out tutoring Tinker altogether, have you? I'm sorry she made such a bad impression when you met her but—''

"She didn't make a bad impression," Eve hurried to assure Gray. "I liked her, and I agree she needs help. I even think I can provide that help if you still want me to, but I sort of got the idea when I came to your house the other day that you weren't quite as eager for me to take on the job as you had been the day before.''

They were sitting across the table from each other, and Gray shifted nervously. If the light hadn't been so dim, she would have thought his face flushed, but that was unlikely. Men his age didn't blush.

"I'm going to be truthful with you, Eve," he said quietly. "You're right, I was having second thoughts. But not for any reason you might think.''

She felt the glow that had permeated her since his call

this afternoon flicker and die. If he no longer wanted her to instruct his child, then why had he phoned and indicated he did? Was he prepared to hire her only because Tinker had asked for her? That thought was a real letdown. Not only was it upsetting to her, but it was also impossible. She had to have the enthusiastic approval of all three members of the family; otherwise, it would just confuse the child.

To say nothing of what it was doing to her!

She felt Gray's hand cover hers where it lay on the table, and his voice was husky when he spoke. "Please, don't misunderstand. Just hear me out."

She was too stunned to speak, but he continued. "I don't know how to say this without taking the risk that you'll think I'm crossing the line between parent and teacher."

She blinked with surprise, but he didn't give her a chance to say anything. "I'm attracted to you, Eve. When I walked into your school last week, it was with the intention of offering an anonymous Ms. Evangeline Costopolous a summer job tutoring my young daughter. But I wasn't prepared for the fascination, the…the pull I felt as I talked to you. When I walked out, I knew I was hooked. And I wasn't happy about it."

Then he'd felt it, too! The excitement between them wasn't just on her side.

Eve opened her mouth, but still no words came out. He removed his hand from hers and gestured with it. "As you know, I've been married and have a daughter. It was never a happy marriage, and it got worse as it went along. The only thing we had going for us was infatuation, and when that wore off there was nothing else to bond us. If it hadn't been for Tinker, we could each have gone our separate ways once we divorced, but our daughter is the glue that binds us now. Now I'm trying to deal with a divorce and child custody. The whole thing has been something of a nightmare, and I learned my lesson. I'm not looking to get seriously involved with a woman again.''

Now Eve was totally confused. "I'm flattered," she said, and felt the radiance returning. "But what does all this have to do with whether or not I tutor Tinker?"

He leaned forward. "Not a thing. Just put it out of your mind. For a while I thought it might not be a good idea to work closely with you, knowing there was this attraction for you on my part. But that's absurd. After all, you're a beautiful and charming woman. You no doubt have a lot of admirers."

Eve didn't know how to reply to that. Did he want her to be his daughter's tutor—or his lover? Both? Or neither? Heaven knows, she was attracted to him, too. And she wasn't any more eager to get involved with him than he was with her. Whatever he had in mind, he was making it clear that it wasn't wedding bells. And she wouldn't accept anything less from any man.

She almost chortled. What was the matter with her? They hadn't even known each other a week yet, and already she was thinking about a proposal of marriage!

She was saved from having to respond to him by their server, who brought the soup course. By silent but mutual consent, they dropped the subject. They chatted about other things: the food, the weather. Finally she was able to bring the conversation around to his personal history.

"Are you a local boy, Gray?" she asked. "Do your parents live here?"

He sipped the delicious beef-and-barley soup they'd both ordered. "Well, yes and no. I was born and raised here until I left to go to the University of California at

Berkeley. After I got my degree, I worked out there for several years, until Dad had a massive heart attack and nearly died.''

"Oh, I'm so sorry,'' Eve said, thinking of her own beloved father. "Did he—that is, is he all right?''

Gray smiled appreciatively. "Yes, but he had to retire as vice-president of the bank, and he can no longer survive the severe winters here, so he and Mom moved to the Rio Grande Valley in southern Texas. There, all he has to do is sit in his orange grove and pick the fruit off his trees.''

Again they were interrupted, this time by the busboy who cleared the empty soup bowls from their table. He was followed shortly by the server with their salads, and by the time they got to the entrée they were more relaxed and at ease with one another—enough so that they were finally able to discuss the subject that had brought them together.

"So, have you made up your mind yet about tutoring Tinker?'' he asked as he cut into his thick piece of meat. "Or have I scared you off with my inappropriate admission? I meant it when I said I'll make a hefty donation to the school roofing fund if you'll agree to take on my daughter.''

"I've given this a lot of thought,'' she admitted, "but before we agree on it, I have to tell you that I'm attracted to you, too.''

This time his eyes widened with surprise, and she hurried on. "However, I'm not any more eager to get involved emotionally than you are, so I don't think we'll have a problem. I've never been married, but I went with a man when I was at the university who wanted all the perks of marriage with none of the commitments. I was naive enough to think I could change his mind, but instead he dumped me."

Even after all this time, she still felt a catch in her throat when she talked about that painful episode. "I was both heartbroken and humiliated, and swore off men forever."

She saw the sympathetic expression on his face, and that was the last thing she wanted. She managed a smile. "Or at least until I grew up enough to be able to tell the good guys from the cads," she amended lightly.

Once again an awkward moment was dispatched by the server who arrived with the dessert menu.

"So," she said when they were again alone. "If you still want me—"

Gray closed his eyes and groaned. "Oh, I want you, all right. Any way I can get you. But for now it will have to be as Tinker's tutor."

Eve's heart pounded, and she couldn't seem to catch her breath. They weren't even touching, yet their conversation was earthshakingly sexy.

"Incidentally, how's the roofing fund coming along?" he asked, suddenly turning the conversation one hundred and eighty degrees.

She cleared her throat and hoped her voice wouldn't tremble. "At the rate donations are coming in, it's going to be years instead of months before we collect enough. However, the donation from you will help," she answered. "We haven't had the money to publicize it broadly enough."

He gazed thoughtfully at her. "Would you like me to speak to the manager at the TV station about possibly doing public service announcements about it?"

Eve gasped, unable to believe what she'd heard. "It would be an immense help!" she exclaimed. "We've been trying to get the newspaper to run a small free ad, but to no avail. Television seemed out of the question.''

She paused to compose herself. ''I'm sure with that kind of publicity, more businesses would make sizable donations. After all, supporting a cause that is good for children is great advertising for them, too.''

He smiled broadly. ''Okay, then I'll speak to Paul Norton, our station manager,'' he promised, then was once again serious. ''You do realize, don't you, that he'll conduct his own investigation before he commits himself?''

She'd agree to almost anything for an opportunity like this. ''Oh, sure, that's no problem. He'll find that everything's on the up and up. Just send him over on a rainy day and he can see for himself,'' she bubbled enthusiastically. ''I don't know how I can ever thank you—''

''No need,'' he interrupted, then took his pen out of his breast pocket to sign the tab. ''It's still early—would you like to go to a movie?''

She looked at her watch, but knew what her answer would have to be. ''Oh, I'm sorry, but I have papers to grade and lesson plans to work on. May I take a raincheck?''

He slid out of the booth. ''For you, anything,'' he promised.

On their way back to her apartment, the elegant sports car seemed even cozier and more intimate than before. Their seats were so close together that his hand inadvertently brushed against her knee when he shifted gears. If she moved her hand mere inches, she could caress his thigh, and the temptation to do so was almost overwhelming.

Maybe taking this job wasn't such a good idea, after all. In fact, she *knew* it wasn't, but didn't seem able to resist.

It was Gray who broke the silence. "When will you be able to start tutoring Tinker?" he asked.

She noticed that he didn't look at her, but stared straight ahead. His voice was somewhat strained. Was he as aware of her as she was of him?

She thought for a minute. "I'd prefer to wait until school is out. That will be this coming Friday, so I can start anytime after that."

He still didn't look at her. "How about Monday?" he suggested.

She was taken aback. "But don't you want her to have a breather before she starts up again?"

He shook his head. "I don't think that's necessary. The longer she's out of school, the harder it will be to get her started again."

Eve was disappointed. She'd hoped to have a little break during which to be lazy, but the sooner she started work, the sooner she'd start getting paid and helping build up the roof fund.

"Monday's fine with me," she told him. "What time do you think would be best?"

"Well... My last broadcast of the day is on the noon news. I'm finished by one, but I can't always leave right away. There's a lot more to forecasting the weather than just reading it on the air. Bambi works from two to six p.m. Would three till five be too late for you?"

Eve thought about it. "Actually, no it isn't. It's late enough that I can have most of the day free, and early enough that if I want to do something in the evening, I can."

He pulled over to the curb and stopped, and she realized that they were already in front of her apartment complex. Gray got out of the car and walked around to open her door. He helped her out and they stood facing each other, but instead of saying good-night there, he took her arm and walked along beside her toward the building.

"Gray, it's not necessary to escort me to my door," she protested, but not vehemently. She loved the extra attention.

"Oh, yes it is," he said with mock seriousness. "My mama taught me to behave like a gentleman. You don't want me to disappoint her, do you?"

Eve giggled. "Oh, my, no. There are too few gentlemen walking around anymore as it is."

They climbed the stairs to the second floor wraparound balcony, and stopped at her door. She'd left the outside light on, and she'd already taken the key from her purse on the way over. She inserted it in the lock and pushed the door open, then turned to face Gray.

"Our station manager is out of town for the next couple of days," he said. "But as soon as he returns, I'll talk to him about the PSAs, then get back to you. Okay?"

"It—it's more than just okay," she told him through the tremble in her voice. "Gray, I can't tell you how much I appreciate your willingness to do this. I don't think even you can understand what a difference the publicity will make to the children, and the teachers, too."

He smiled. "I'm glad I can help, but you must understand that it will be up to Paul. All I can do is make him aware of the need."

"That's more than enough," she said thickly. "If you can get his ear, I guarantee you I'll win over his heart."

"I don't doubt that for a moment," he assured her gravely.

She took a deep breath and put out her hand. "Thank you for the wonderful evening." Her voice was low and husky; she hadn't planned it that way—that's just the way it came out.

"I can't remember ever having such a delightful time," she continued. "Or such a delicious dinner…"

Slowly, gently he put his hands on either side of her throat and tipped her face up, then placed one thumb across her mouth in a hushing motion. Her heart stopped beating and she forgot to breathe.

"It's much too soon," he murmured, and his voice was as hoarse as hers had been. "and I promised myself I'd behave, but there's one thing I have to know."

As he gently caressed her nape, unable to stop herself, she leaned forward until they were almost touching. Her knees shook; her lips trembled as the tip of her tongue slowly moistened them.

His fingers dug into her shoulders. "Do you want to kiss me as much as I want to kiss you?"

"Oh, yes." Her answer was unhesitating as she closed the slim gap between them and walked into his arms.

Chapter Four

Gray held Eve loosely around the waist with one arm and twined the fingers of his other hand through her thick dark curls, then lowered his head and brushed her lips with his—once, and then again.

His embrace was strong but gentle, and his breath was fresh, like the breeze from the sea. She snuggled closer, and he raised his head and guided hers to his shoulder, then rubbed his cheek in her hair.

"You're as soft and warm as I knew you'd be," he murmured into her ear.

For a moment they just stood there, and she reveled in his gentle grasp. Then he was the one to pull away. She felt chilly and bereft without his arms around her, and she leaned back against the doorjamb to support herself, to keep her trembling knees from buckling.

He put his fingers under her chin and lifted her head so their eyes met. Again he captured her mouth, this time in a slow, tender but overwhelming kiss. Then he turned and walked away, leaving her reeling in the doorway.

* * *

Gray floated along the balcony and down the stairs, his head in the clouds and his feet hardly touching the floor. What kind of magic had this beautiful young charmer woven around him? No other woman had ever affected him this way. Kissing her was like kissing an angel—soft as a baby and radiant as the glow of heaven.

There was nothing earthy about it, although he knew beyond doubt there would be if it ever happened again. He'd better enjoy this moment, because it was a one-time thing. He'd see to that.

Eve watched Gray as he walked away from her and descended the stairs. Her legs were so rubbery that she slid slowly down the doorjamb and sat on the threshold, her knees bent and her arms wrapped around her shins. She'd known that a kiss between the two of them would be special, but she hadn't been prepared for the exultation that swept over her and left her totally enthralled.

It hadn't even been a passionate kiss. It had been sweet and pure and tender, but with an undercurrent of yearning. The kind of kiss that would never burn out, but would keep some lucky woman wrapped in a cloak of adoration forever.

Eve didn't hear from Gray again until Saturday, although her nervous system had been attuned to quiver at the ring of the doorbell or the sound of the telephone. She was well aware that he hadn't said anything about talking to her again until after he'd asked his station manager about the public service spots, and he'd made it plain that the station manager wouldn't be available for several days. Still, she'd thought that after that kiss…

She mentally tried to brush that thought from her mind. Obviously "that kiss" hadn't affected him as it had her.

So why was she surprised by that? He'd taken great pains to let her know that although he was attracted to her, he was a committed bachelor. If he was as forthright with all the women he dated as he'd been with her, he probably had lots of them in this town, sitting by their telephones after a night of passion, hoping he'd call them even though they knew there would be no lasting relationship.

On this bright and sunny Saturday morning, Eve was sitting at the table sipping a mug of coffee and working on a crossword puzzle. This was the first day of her summer vacation and she was determined to loll around all day, doing only what she wanted to. That included starting the new Stephen King novel that she knew would scare the daylights out of her, but that she nonetheless looked forward to with anticipation.

She raised her arms in a long, leisurely stretch, then stood up. First, though, she'd better do a load of wash. She could take her book with her to the communal laundry room downstairs, and read while the machines were running.

She gathered all her dirty clothes and linen into a basket and was on her way to the front door, when the doorbell chimed. As usual her muscles twitched, and an image of Gray sprang to mind. She forced herself to relax. No way would this be him. For one thing, it was a weekend. He probably had Tinker. Even if he didn't, he was too considerate to pop in on her without calling first.

With her basket of clothes under one arm, she hurried to the door and opened it.

It *was* Gray! And Tinker wasn't with him.

"Gray!" she exclaimed. "I wasn't expecting you... That is, please, come in."

Balancing the filled basket on her hip, she fumbled to unlock the screen door.

"I know you weren't," he said as he waited. "I'm sorry, but I couldn't call you. Your phone seemed to be out of order. I reported it, but the phone company said they were having a problem with the lines in this area, so since I couldn't get through, I decided to take a chance and just drop by. If it's inconvenient—"

"No, no. Not at all," she lied, and pushed the screen open. Actually, it *was* inconvenient, or at least embarrassing. If she'd known he was coming, she'd have dressed up instead of pulling on her comfortable old jeans that had faded and shrunk with numerous washings and now clung to her like second skin.

"I was just on my way to do laundry," she explained unnecessarily as she backed up to let him enter, all the while aware of the ratty old sweatshirt she was wearing. It should have been tossed out years ago.

In just one minute, she'd undone the impression she'd worked so hard to achieve last time she saw him—that of an attractive, cool, and sophisticated career woman. After today, the only lasting impression he'd have of her was that of a slob with too-tight pants, tousled hair and a messy apartment.

"Don't let me disrupt your schedule," he said as he hesitated at the open door. "I can come back another time—"

"There's nothing urgent about washing clothes," she said as she set her basket on the floor next to the sofa. "Come in and have a cup of coffee."

"Well, if you're sure..." he said, then walked in and shut the door behind him.

Gray followed Eve into the kitchen. He'd forced himself to stay away from her these past five days, but finally he couldn't stand it any longer. He'd broken every self-imposed rule he'd set for himself concerning her, and followed his longing instead of his good sense. Now he was enjoying every second of watching that curvy bottom of hers move enticingly from side to side in those clinging jeans that left little to the imagination.

He was suddenly aware of his throbbing arousal. Man! He wasn't prepared for this strong a reaction, but perhaps that was because he'd been hiding from the truth of it. When he'd taken her to dinner, she'd been beautiful with a natural elegance that gave him permission to look but not touch. Today, she seemed so much more approachable.

He'd told himself that he could handle his attraction. That for Tinker's sake, they could control their mutual feelings for one another and just be friends. But that was before he saw her in tight pants that showed off her long, slender legs, her thighs that joined her hips in a most inviting fashion.

He couldn't even tear his gaze away. How was he supposed to keep his hands off her?

She stopped at a table situated at the far end of the rectangular kitchen. The morning newspaper was strewn around on it, and she quickly gathered it up and began folding it. "Sorry about the mess," she apologized. "Go ahead and sit down. I'll bring the coffee."

He could see that she was distressed about the house not being pristine, and he tried to put her at ease. "You call this a mess?" he said with a chuckle. "You should see mine. I have a cleaning woman who comes in once a week, but the other six days I'm pretty slovenly."

She smiled, and he could feel an easing of the tension

in the atmosphere. "Now that's not true, and I know it's not because I've been to your house. Remember? It was spotless."

He chuckled. "Yeah, and that was the day the cleaning lady came."

They both laughed. Eve picked up the filled mug and carried it to the table, then sat down with him. He was also dressed casually, but his jeans and T-shirt were a lot newer and in better condition than were her clothes.

This was the first time she'd seen him in anything but a suit, and it was evident he'd look great in anything he chose to wear. The muscles under the sleeves of his T-shirt were proof of regular workouts. He might have a sedentary job, but his body was hard and rugged. She wondered if he'd ever done any modeling, but decided not to bring up that subject. It was best not to get too personal. Much more of these thoughts, and she'd throw herself at him and beg for another of his bone-melting kisses!

"So, what was it you wanted to talk to me about?" she asked instead.

"I wanted to tell you I spoke with Paul Norton, our station manager, about doing public service announcements for you," Gray told her. "He seemed interested. Said he'd check it out, and if everything is the way I've presented it to him he'd run it past the legal department. If they approve, it's a go."

A hot rush of gratitude swept through her, and she could feel the glow that radiated from her face as she impulsively grabbed his hand and brought it to her mouth. "Oh, Gray, how can I ever thank you," she said between the kisses she was planting on his palm and wrist.

It was just a gesture of appreciation, she told herself,

but before she realized what was happening, he'd pulled her from her chair and set her on his lap. "If you want to do that, then be prepared for the consequences," he muttered hoarsely, and brought his mouth down on hers.

Without another thought, she wrapped her arms around his neck and gave as well as she was getting.

This time was different: he didn't hold her as if she were a piece of fragile porcelain that would break. He held her the way he would embrace a desirable woman whom he wanted to know better, needed to know more intimately. A woman he hungered for just as she hungered for him.

Even as his hands roamed over her, gently but eagerly, she could feel the effort he was making to hold back. She was both grateful and disappointed. She wanted to know the full force of his passion, but it would be foolish to encourage that. It could so easily get out of control, and neither of them wanted a commitment.

His hand cupped her breast, and he rained small kisses over her face. She whimpered with excitement and snuggled closer in his lap as she tightened her arms around his neck and nuzzled his throat. She could feel his unyielding hardness under her bottom, and gloried in it. It gave her a delicious sense of gratification to know that she could affect him so strongly.

A sound like a mixture of pleasure and pain escaped from deep in his throat, and he laid his cheek against her breast. "I promised myself this wasn't going to happen," he said raggedly.

"Are you sorry?" she whispered in his ear.

"Not right now," he said. "But I will be when I have to put you away from me. Then I'm going to suffer, for sure."

"So will I," she admitted, and she realized that although he'd been caressing her ribs, back and breasts through her sweatshirt, he'd never once let his hand stray below her waist or under her clothes.

He was obviously determined not to seduce her, even though he could have done so with little effort. She'd never been this...*ready* for a man before. She knew he was the one exhibiting good sense, even though part of her wished he wouldn't.

Gradually, Gray slowed his exploration of Eve's upper body and settled on her ample breasts. They were high and soft, but he could feel her hardened nipples even through the shirt she wore.

He ached to tear off the offending garment and take those delicious peaks in his mouth. To suckle them and drink of her sweetness.

She shifted in his lap, sending tremors through him. It took all his strength and resolve, but he managed to find the willpower to push her away from him and sit her upright on his thighs. "Sorry, luv," he groaned, "but if we don't cool it now, we won't be able to later."

Would that really be so bad? Eve wondered as she struggled to catch her breath and gain some semblance of composure. Obviously he thought it would, and she wasn't going to make a fool of herself by protesting.

"Yes, you're right," she agreed instead. "I'm... I'm sorry. I don't usually—"

"I know you don't," he interrupted to assure her, possibly a tad too fast to be believable. Was he trying to cover up a suspicion that she made love with every good-looking man who came to her door? She wouldn't blame him if he did think that. She hadn't given him any reason to believe otherwise.

She felt a hot flush suffuse her face, and quickly stood up. Gray rose, too, and for a moment they just stood there, looking anywhere but at each other. Neither of them seemed willing or able to break the awkward silence.

Finally, Gray spoke. "Eve, I'm the one who should apologize. I didn't come here to…to—"

"Why don't we just agree that we were both out of line," she suggested quickly, wishing he'd just go away and leave her to crawl under the bed and hide. "Now, if you don't mind, I really do have to get back to my laundry…"

"Yes, of course," he said, then hesitated. "There's just one other thing. Are there any supplies I'll need to buy for Tinker before you start tutoring her on Monday?"

Eve's eyes widened with alarm. Tinker! Monday! After today's encounter, how could she possible work with the child every weekday afternoon in Gray's home?

On the other hand, how could she not? She'd agreed to do it. Tinker was expecting her, and Gray was relying on her. Besides, if she backed out now, he'd know how badly he'd humiliated her, even though he was trying to protect her from her own naiveté.

She took a deep breath and turned to face him. "No, it will be easier if I pick up what's needed and then bill you. Is there a limit on what I can spend on books, supplies?"

"None whatsoever," he said as she started edging them toward the front door.

She quickened her pace. "Okay then, I'll see Tinker on Monday. Let her wear comfortable clothes, and the first day or so will be mostly a get-acquainted time while we work up to the lessons."

"May I be there for a little while?" he asked as they reached the door.

She frowned as she grabbed the knob and opened it. That was the last thing she wanted, but… "Well, it's your house and your daughter—"

"That's not what I meant," he growled. "It's probably hard for you to believe after what just happened, but I'm not planning to attack you, Eve. I'd just like to observe for a short time to see how Tinker reacts to the new arrangement."

Eve bit her lip as she silently cursed herself. "That's not what I meant, either," she said apologetically. "Of course, you can be there. Actually, it would probably be a good way to help ease the tension Tinker might feel with a new teacher."

He stepped outside, then turned. "All right then, I'll stay around for a few minutes just to see how things go. And, Eve— thanks for agreeing to tutor her."

Now he was doing it again. Charming her with that little smile filled with gratitude and those blue eyes brimming with admiration. How could she resist him?

Before she could respond, he'd walked away.

By Monday, Eve was a nervous wreck. She'd spent the weekend reliving that brief interlude with Gray in her kitchen and being alternately thrilled and disconcerted. What had gotten into her? Gray was practically a stranger, and what little relationship they had was—should be— strictly business.

So why had she gone willingly—no, *fervently*—into his arms and melted all over him? Not only that, but she'd started it!

Even the thought of the way she'd behaved made her squirm. He'd been a perfect gentleman up until the time she'd shamelessly thrown herself at him! She'd asked for what happened next, and although he seemed to be enjoying it as much as she, he was the one who put a stop to it. If he hadn't, she was almost sure she'd have made love with him.

She'd dithered about this meeting with him all weekend, dreading it. And now here she was, pulling up to the curb in front of his home fifteen minutes early! Oh well, there was nothing she could do about that now. She might as well go in and get that first agonizing meeting over with, so she could put it out of her mind and concentrate on making a friend of Tinker.

She gathered up her purse and the leather briefcase—the one her parents had given her last fall when she first started teaching—and got out of the car. Gray's red Jaguar was nowhere to be seen. He probably kept it in the garage, but there was a fairly new shiny white Toyota Cresida parked in the driveway.

Did he have two cars? Or maybe he had company. A girlfriend?

She shook her head and fought back a stab of jealousy. Obviously it was none of her business, but she preferred not to have a lot of people around when she was trying to instruct a child. Gray had known she was coming. He'd even indicated that he'd like to be here for a while, too. So why would he invite someone else?

A disturbing thought occurred to her. Did he think he needed a chaperon to protect himself from her unbridled ardor!

She rang the bell and waited. A stereo from inside the house was playing loud music. Elvis Presley, she thought, although the singer had been before her time.

Thinking the people inside couldn't hear the bell above the music, she punched it again, harder this time. In only a moment the door opened, and Tinker stood on the other side of the storm door.

She recognized Eve and let her in. "Come in," she said.

"Hello, Tinker." Eve greeted her as she stepped across the threshold and shut both doors.

The youngster was dressed in khaki slacks with a brown-and-green plaid, flannel shirt that wasn't tucked in at the waist. South Dakota can be pretty chilly in late May and early June, and this was one of those periods. Eve was also wearing slacks: black, with a black-and-white diamond-patterned pullover sweater.

"Who is it, sweetie?" called a girlish voice over the din. But the person who appeared from the direction of the living room to stand beside Tinker was not a girl. She was a small, perfectly proportioned woman, who wore a long black skirt and white Victorian-style blouse, and was possibly one of the most beautiful women Eve had ever seen.

Her features were exquisite, like those of a doll crafted of the most delicate porcelain. The feeling of being awkward and plain that had tormented Eve from her childhood swept over her again. Even though she knew she'd outgrown her adolescent ungainliness, the feeling was no less painful now than it had been then.

"It's Ms. Cost—Costop..." The child stumbled over the unfamiliar pronunciation.

"I'm Eve Costopoulos." She introduced herself and put out her hand.

"And I'm *Mrs.* Flint, Tinker's mother."

Eve didn't miss the emphasis on the title, *Mrs.* Not Ms., or Bambi, but *Mrs.* The woman was sending Eve a message that came through loud and clear. *This man is mine, and woe betide anyone who tries to interfere.*

The other woman barely touched Eve's hand with her own, then dropped it. "Oh, you must be the teacher my husband hired to tutor our daughter." She wrinkled her small, slightly turned-up nose in a gesture of disapproval. "Not that she needs it, you understand. There's nothing wrong with her intelligence. She just doesn't make enough of an effort—"

"Oh, Mother..." Tinker protested. Eve immediately picked up on Tinker's pained flush, as well as the *my husband* jab. Had Gray been lying to her? Were he and Bambi still married? But that didn't make sense. If so, and he was the philandering type and didn't want Bambi to know he was coming on to Eve, why would he hire Eve to tutor his daughter? His secret wouldn't be safe for very long under those conditions.

Bambi's attitude toward Tinker was even more pressing, though, and she needed straightening out right now. "Mrs. Flint, pardon me for interrupting, but I was given to understand that Tinker is dyslexic."

"Well, that's what the reading specialists say," Bambi said petulantly. "But I'm sure that if she'd apply herself a little more, pay attention in class, she could do the work just fine."

For heaven's sake, where was Gray? How could Eve be expected to deal alone with the Flint family's problems? She wasn't a psychologist—just a tutor.

"Are you saying you don't want her tutored?" Eve asked. "If so, I'll leave now—"

"No, don't!" Bambi said sharply, and Eve was sure she'd detected alarm in her tone. "That is, I don't feel it's necessary, but neither do I want to go against *my husband's* wishes. He's such a dear. Always looking out for Tinker's and my best interests."

Well, bully for him! Eve thought sarcastically. Her temper continued to simmer.

"Personally, I think it's a waste of time and money,"

Bambi continued. "But Gray insists it's necessary, so I'll go along."

Just then, Eve heard a key being turned in the lock and managed to step aside just before the door behind her opened.

"Whoops, sorry," Gray apologized. "I didn't know anyone was standing so close..."

He paused and looked at the small group of people assembled there, then glared at Bambi. "What are you doing here? Where's Judy?"

"Oh, I sent the baby-sitter home," she said airily. "I wanted to meet Tinker's teacher, so I told them at the restaurant that I had a migraine and needed to go home."

Eve was shocked that Bambi would brag about lying to her employers in front of her impressionable daughter.

Gray took a deep breath. He looked annoyed with the woman, too, but he spoke calmly to Eve. "I'm really sorry about this, Eve. I was called back to the station about an hour ago, but I thought I'd be home before you got here. I told the baby-sitter to tell you that if I wasn't here, I would be shortly, and to go ahead and start getting acquainted with Tinker."

He eyed her thoughtfully. "Did you get my message?" His tone was edgy, and she wasn't sure whether he was upset with his ex-wife—wife?—or with her.

"There hasn't been time, Gray," Eve answered. "I just got here a few minutes ahead of you. I hadn't even realized you weren't in the house."

He uttered a somewhat neutral sound that could have indicated belief or disbelief, then asked, "Have you two met?"

"We introduced ourselves," Bambi said quickly. "Now, I've got coffee all made, so why don't you all go on into the living room and get comfortable while I fetch it.''

She turned to Tinker. "Sweetie pie, you can come and help me carry the things out.''

She and Tinker took off through the dining room and into the kitchen, while Gray and Eve headed for the living room. Gray was now clearly irritated.

"I'm sorry, Eve," he said again. "I had no idea Bambi was going to be here—''

Eve couldn't hold back any longer. "Where does she live?''

He looked surprised, but answered, "She lives up the street and around the corner on Cherry Tree Lane—why?''

That couldn't be more than a block or two away! If they couldn't get along well enough to stay married, then why live in houses that were so close to each other? Were they divorced but sleeping together whenever the urge struck? She had to find out if he was being truthful with her.

"Gray, before we go any further, I need to know what your relationship with Bambi is.''

He blinked in what looked like astonishment. "I've already told you, we're divorced.''

"Then why did she introduce herself as *Mrs. Flint,* and refer to you as her *husband?''*

Gray groaned, but Eve was too overwrought to notice. "There's something you need to know about me, Gray," she said angrily, before he could answer. "In spite of the way I behaved Saturday, I don't get involved with married men.''

The color drained from his face, but she was too furious to care. "I'm not the type for casual relationships. I was

raised in the Greek culture, and we have strongly in-
grained family values.''

"So do I," he protested. "Eve, if you'll just let me
talk, I can explain—"

But unfortunately he couldn't, because just then Bambi
and Tinker came with the coffee. Bambi picked up the
silver coffeepot and started to pour, but Eve stood up.
She'd had all of this situation she could handle.

"I'm sorry, but I won't be able to stay," she said,
reaching for her purse.

"But surely you can have some coffee," Bambi said,
looking pleased.

"Eve!" Gray was also standing. "I want to talk to
you."

"There's really no need," she said, cutting him off and
heading for the door, trying to get out of there before she
blew up and created a scene that would upset Tinker.

Tinker! She'd forgotten all about the child's feelings in
this. The least she could do was tell her goodbye.

She stopped and gazed around the room, finally spot-
ting the youngster silently huddled on the hearth, looking
lonely and forlorn. Eve's heart went out to her, and she
went back to hunker down in front of her.

"Goodbye, Tinker," she said, and couldn't resist reaching out to brush an unruly lock of hair off the little girl's
cheek.

Tinker blinked, and Eve saw the glint of tears in her
eyes. "I thought you were going to be my new teacher,"
she said, and her voice shook slightly.

"I—I..." Eve was at a loss for words. How could she
explain a triangle like this to an eight-year-old? Especially
when she was the focus of the dispute.

Were Gray and Bambi just using Tinker and her in a
spiteful game of one-upmanship to shift the blame for

their marriage having gone sour? And why had Eve let them do it? She should have followed her strong instincts and never gotten involved with Gray Flint in the first place.

The whole situation was unthinkable! Why were three supposedly intelligent adults putting a child in the middle of such an impossible situation? Tinker was much too young to handle it. Especially since she'd already been subjected to the trauma of her parents' separation— whether it was divorce or just estrangement.

"You don't want to teach me, do you?" Tinker said. "You know I'm too dumb to learn. That I'll never be smart like other kids."

Gray and Bambi gasped, and there was a wrenching sob followed by the release of tears cascading down Tinker's pale cheeks. Eve couldn't restrain herself any longer. She engulfed the little girl in her arms and held her.

Chapter Five

"**O**h, honey, no!" Eve assured her. "That's not true. You're not dumb!" Eve hated that word, but it was the one Tinker used and understood. "Actually, you're very bright. You'd have to be to have come as far as you have in your studies even though you were born with a learning problem that makes it harder for you than it is for most children. Your mom and dad have told you about that, and you've pretty well overcome it now."

Tinker clung to Eve and sniffled. "Then why do I still have so much trouble?"

Eve's arms tightened around her. "Because you're not ready to do third-grade work yet. We'll have to go back to the first-grade level and catch up on all that you've missed."

Eve knew the minute she heard herself say "we" that she'd botched it, and she wasn't wrong. Tinker pulled back and looked at her. "Then you *are* going to teach me?"

Eve closed her eyes and groaned. "Oh, Tinker, I didn't mean—"

The child pulled out of Eve's embrace. "Then you haven't been telling me the truth. You do think I'm dumb, and you don't want to teach me."

Eve got to her feet. "No, honey, that's not what I mean," she said shakily as she looked around the room for Gray. Why didn't he help her out?

She spotted him standing by the hallway where she'd left him, and he must have misinterpreted her expression because he addressed his daughter's declaration. "Tinker, you're being rude. It's not polite to tell Ms. Costopoulos what she thinks. You can't know that. Now tell her you're sorry."

Now Eve felt even worse. She hadn't meant for Gray to scold the youngster. She'd just wanted him to help her come up with a good excuse not to tutor Tinker. He must know she couldn't teach his daughter if by doing so it caused friction between her parents.

Tinker blinked back tears again and looked at the floor. "I'm sorry, I—" Her voice broke and she started again. "But if I'm not dumb, then why can't you tutor me?"

"She has a good point, Eve," Gray said, much to her surprise and chagrin. "Can't we at least discuss it?"

Discuss it? What good would that do? The whole idea was impossible. Surely, he could see that. Why would he want her to tutor Tinker when he knew it would upset Bambi?

Her hesitation must have encouraged him, and he continued. "You'd scheduled the next two hours to spend with Tinker, so why not spend them with me, instead?"

He glared at Bambi. "Since Bambi has decided to take the rest of the day off, she can take Tinker on home, and we can have a little privacy to try to sort this thing out. Okay?"

Bambi looked mutinous. "No, it's not okay," she interrupted as though he'd been addressing his remarks to her. "I'm Tinker's mother. I have a say in this."

Gray looked at Tinker, then at Eve, and back to Bambi. "All right," he said. "If that's what you want. You and I will talk in the office." He motioned for her to precede him down the hall.

Bambi hung back, obviously displeased. "Why can't we do it right here?"

"Do you want to talk to me, or not?" he growled, making it plain that it would be his way or not at all. Obviously he had no intention of arguing with his unreasonable ex-wife in front of their daughter and his guest.

A few seconds after Gray and Bambi disappeared down the hall, the sound of the door shutting broke the brief silence. Eve and Tinker looked at each other, at a loss for words. Eve cleared her throat and looked around.

"Your dad has a lovely home," she commented.

Tinker nodded. "It's okay, but you should see mine and Mom's. It's bigger and has an upstairs. My grandma used to live with us, but she died."

"Oh, I'm so sorry," Eve murmured.

That must have been Bambi's mother, since Gray had said his parents lived in Texas.

"I miss her," Tinker said, and there was sadness in her voice. "She used to sew dresses for me, and for my dolls. She baked cookies and pies, too, and she never called me stupid or lazy like my mom does when she tries to help me with my homework."

That last sentence made Eve uncomfortable about the way the conversation was going. Although her first inclination was to jump to Tinker's defense, she'd always thought it reprehensible to solicit gossip about family members from an unsuspecting child, and she wasn't going to do it now.

Instead, she cast around for another subject. "Why don't you tell me what you've been studying in school? What are your favorite storybooks?"

Tinker didn't seem to mind talking about her schooling, and a short time later Gray and Bambi rejoined them, both looking out of sorts. Apparently theirs was not as amicable a divorce as Bambi had implied earlier.

Gray fastened his attention on Tinker as he walked to the closet door and took out a windbreaker. "Put this on, baby. You're going home with your mom now, but we'll talk again tomorrow."

He helped her into the jacket, and they hugged and kissed.

When he'd finished with his daughter, he took out another coat and helped Bambi into it. With her, he was polite but impersonal. Neither one spoke to the other. He didn't look or act like a man who was pining for his ex-wife.

Eve had been standing in the living room, facing the entryway and hall, her back to the fireplace. When Gray turned and came toward her, she could see the lines of tension in his face, and the frustration in his eyes.

"I'm so sorry about this, Eve," he apologized. "I had no inkling Bambi was going to show up and make a scene. I should have expected it, though. I don't know why I'm always surprised when she pulls these nasty little stunts."

Eve couldn't help feeling sorry for him. He looked so beaten down. Ordinarily, it would have been none of her business and she wouldn't ask questions, but by bringing her into the midst of this donnybrook with his ex-wife, he'd made it Eve's problem, too. She was entitled to know what was going on.

"Are you telling me the truth about being divorced from her, Gray?"

"Yes," he said, and held up his hand. "I swear. I have the papers to prove it if you want to see them."

"That won't be necessary," she said quickly, embarrassed that he felt he had to offer.

"I can understand why she still calls herself 'Mrs. Flint,' but why does she keep referring to you as 'my husband'? It wasn't just a slip—she did it several times, and very deliberately."

He shook his head and took her by the arm, sending waves of warmth up and down it. "Come, let's sit down," he said, and guided her to the couch where they both settled themselves comfortably.

Gray started to reach for the silver coffeepot, but then paused. "The coffee's still warm, but could I interest you in something a little stronger?"

He looked as if he could use a shot of whiskey or brandy, and she nodded. "Wine would be fine with me. I'm not much of a drinker, but please feel free to have whatever you prefer."

He smiled. "Wine's fine with me, too. Is Merlot okay?"

"Great," she said as he got up and went into the kitchen, returning a few minutes later with a carafe of red wine and two sparkling crystal glasses.

He set the smaller tray next to the bigger one on the long coffee table and poured the ruby liquid, then handed one glass to Eve and took the other for himself.

They both settled back again and took a sip of their drinks. "Now," Gray said with a sigh, "where were we? Ah yes, Bambi's insistence on referring to me as her hus-

band. It's just her way of annoying me. You see, she
didn't want the divorce, although she didn't fight it very
hard once she was assured I'd continue to support her as
well as Tinker.''

Eve blinked. ''But she works…''

''Yeah, she does now, but only part-time. She and another woman split the dinner-hour shift. When we first
met, she was a receptionist in my dentist's office. She's
good with people—bubbly and amicable with that childish
vulnerability that makes them want to take care of her.''

He hesitated as though reminiscing. ''Actually, that's
what drew me to her, and I didn't realize there was nothing behind that facade until it was too late. I wanted a
woman, and she wanted an adoring knight in shining ar-
mor.''

He grimaced. ''We were married just two months after
we met, and that was a mistake. It's not nearly enough
time to get to know someone and find out if you're com-
patible before taking the big step.''

He cleared his throat. ''By the time we'd both decided
the marriage wasn't going to work, we found out she was
pregnant. Neither of us wanted our child to be the product
of a broken home, so we declared a truce. She quit her
job to stay home and take care of the baby, and didn't
work again until six years later, when we finally had to
admit we were totally incompatible and filed for divorce.''

He looked thoughtful. ''In the interval, she liked being
the wife of a TV personality, even if it was just the weatherman. She gave parties and got involved in charity work,
stuff like that.''

He leaned forward and poured more wine into his
empty glass, then held the carafe out to her. But she shook
her head; her glass was still half full.

"She didn't want a vocation," he said, almost to himself. "She's always needed someone to take care of her."

A thought niggled at Eve and she voiced it. "If she's unable or unwilling to take care of herself, how did she ever get custody of Tinker?"

"Joint custody," Grant corrected. "I agreed to it. I firmly believe that a child needs both a mother and a father, and we had these two houses just around the corner from each other.

"We'd originally bought this one as an investment, so when we separated, I moved in and let Bambi have the larger one. She prevailed upon her widowed mother to come and live with her and Tinker after I moved out. Margie was a wonderful woman, and I knew she'd keep Bambi in line and see to it that Tinker was well taken care of when I couldn't be there."

"She must be the 'grandma' Tinker told me about who died," Eve commented.

Gray ran his fingers through his hair. "Yes, she was. She died very suddenly a few months ago of a heart attack. I'm sure that's why Bambi is being so possessive of me now. She lost her mother, and she's afraid she'll lose my support, both financial and emotional, too."

Eve thought of her own cherished mother, and felt a pang of anguish at the thought of losing her. A tide of compassion for Bambi washed away some of the censure that had tainted her impression of the woman.

Gray took another sip of his wine and set the glass down. "Eve, I want you to understand one thing. I'm not going to let Bambi's obstinate self-centeredness interfere with my daughter's education. Tinker *will* be tutored this summer so she can start school next fall on the same level as her classmates. I just hope you will agree to be the one to teach her. She likes you, and you're eminently qualified. Please, say you'll do it.''

Eve cupped her glass in both hands and watched the twinkle of light playing off the crystal. She believed him. There was no reason not to. She also agreed with him. It would be wrong to deny Tinker the help she so desperately needed just because her mother was exhibiting a streak of childish jealousy.

She looked up and found Gray watching her closely. How could she refuse him? His voice was stilled, but his eyes pleaded with her. It would take someone stronger than she to resist, and, besides, it was important for Tinker's sake.

She sighed. ''All right, if you can square it with her mother, I'll do it, but it's imperative that Bambi approve and let Tinker *know* she approves. Otherwise, we'll just be wasting my time and your money. I can't build up her self-confidence when her mother just tears it down—''

She hadn't meant to allude to the fact that Bambi called her daughter ''dumb'' and ''lazy.'' It was too late now, though. Gray had picked up on it and was gaping at her.

''What do you mean?'' he demanded. ''What has Bambi done now? Do you know something I don't?''

Eve cursed her motor-mouth, but it was too late to back down. ''Oh, damn, I'm sorry. I didn't mean to bring that up until I was sure—''

''Bring what up?'' Gray interrupted. ''Is something going on that I should know?''

Eve put her wineglass down, afraid of spilling it. ''I'm not sure, Gray,'' she said, then recounted what Tinker had told her while he and Bambi were in the office.

Gray listened carefully, then shook his head. ''I think that's been taken care of.'' He sounded tired and discouraged. ''Bambi did start scolding and taunting Tinker while her mother was living with them, and Margie put a stop to it. But Bambi may have started up again. She's so impatient with Tinker's learning difficulties. I'll check into it and see what's going on."

"I'm sorry," Eve said. "I didn't mean to tattle—"

"Tattle all you feel is necessary," he instructed her. "I need to know these things. I can't trust Bambi to act like an adult. She's so immature. It's like raising two children by myself. I need a lot of help."

Eve smiled. "You're doing just fine, so shall we try again tomorrow to get this act together? I assume you can handle Bambi?"

He chortled. "Don't be too sure, but I'll do my damndest. I think she understands from that little talk we had in the office that I won't put up with any more of her shenanigans. I'm going to count on you to let me know if Tinker shows any signs that things aren't going well at home."

Eve hated being put in that position, but still, it was part of a teacher's job to protect her students if she suspected they were being mistreated. Not that Bambi would do anything to injure her daughter physically, but she could damage Tinker's spirit with hurtful, unthinking remarks.

"Yes, Gray, I will," she assured him, then reached for her purse. "Now I'd better get home and do my laundry—"

She stopped, paralyzed with embarrassment as she remembered the last time she and Gray had discussed her laundry. She felt a hot wash of color suffuse her face and was tempted to hide it in her hands. No matter what she said, it would be the wrong thing.

When she got up the nerve to look at him, he appeared similarly flustered, but there was a longing in his glance that couldn't be missed. Was she sending him the same message? She had to be, because her feelings were too strong to hide.

For a moment they just looked at each other, their gazes tender and clinging. Then he reached out and put his hand on her cheek. His palm was warm and gentle, and he moved it slowly to run his long slender fingers through the unruly locks of her hair.

He was mesmerizing her; there was no other word for it. She couldn't break the magnetism of the passion their eyes generated when locked in this tender position. Nor did she want to.

She scooted closer to him, and his fingers stopped caressing her hair and moved to cup her chin and lift her face to his. She closed her eyes as he kissed first one lid and then the other.

"I've been so hungry for you," he whispered. "I've been in torment—wanting you, needing you, but terrified of scaring you away."

"You could never do that," she murmured as she inched her palms up his chest and clasped her hands behind his neck.

She felt him shiver. "Oooh, that feels so good," he said shakily. "How long do I have to wait until I can kiss you again?"

For answer, she captured his mouth and sucked lightly on his lower lip. Any resistance either of them may have planned drained away as their arms tightened and their mouths joined in a warm sensual surrender.

He cupped the sides of her breasts, and she raised her head so he could rain kisses on her throat. She let her hands roam over his shoulders and back.

"What is that scent you're wearing?" he murmured

against her hair. "It seems familiar, but I can't quite place it."

She laughed softly and buried her face in the side of his neck. "You should be able to. It's called Apple."

"That's it," he said triumphantly, and hugged her. "Cinnamon apple pie! How could I have failed to recognize it? You'd better be careful with that stuff, sweetheart. Don't you know hot cinnamon apple pie à la mode drives men crazy? They'll do anything for a bite."

She worried his earlobe with her teeth. "Does that include you, too?"

"That includes me, especially," he growled. He fastened his mouth on her neck and sucked, gently at first, then more strongly.

The sexual pull all the way from Eve's neck to her insides nearly sent her into orbit, and she moaned and stiffened in his arms. She'd never experienced anything like this before.

He immediately released her. "What? Did I hurt you?"

"No, of course not," she said, and hoped her embarrassment didn't show. "It's just that I..." Well, hell, she might as well admit it. "I liked it."

He smiled, obviously pleased. "So did I," he whispered, then took her back in his arms, tilted her head to get the maximum enjoyment, and kissed her, long and tenderly and with a rising tide of ardor that left them both breathless. Then Gray broke it off and cradled her head on his shoulder.

Eve was surprised. She knew that he was aroused, and she'd admitted that she was, but he apparently had no intention of going any further in their lovemaking. She appreciated his consideration for her—but it was driving her crazy.

* * *

Gray was having a hard time controlling himself. His whole body was in turmoil. What in hell was the matter with him? All the time he'd been holding Eve, savoring her softness and basking in the sweet melody of that husky voice that could recite the alphabet and still be sexy, danger signals had been flashing in his mind. Wherever he touched her, it excited him even more. Her breasts were full and high, and he wanted to pull off her sweater and bra and stroke those breasts with his bare palms.

He was an idiot to keep putting himself through this. He knew better than to get close to her, let alone touch her, and still he couldn't resist. When they were apart, all he could think of was getting together again; when they were together, he couldn't keep his hands off her. All he knew was how much he wanted her—and not only in his bed.

That's what scared the hell out of him. If he wasn't careful, he was going to get in over his head with a girl whom he'd have sworn was too young, too immature, too vulnerable to appeal to him.

So why had he pursued her so vigorously? Why hadn't he simply taken no for an answer the first time she'd said it, and moved along?

Because he hadn't been able to deny himself the pleasure of her company, that's why. She'd smiled at him, and he was lost. Now he was about to make another mistake. He knew that's what it was, and he was also going into it with his eyes wide open.

He rubbed his cheek in her fragrant hair. "Have dinner with me," he murmured. "I can fix something here, or we can order out. That is, unless you'd rather go to a restaurant."

Eve didn't respond right away, and as he held his breath Gray was sure she was going to refuse his invitation. He'd

been foolish to issue it. After he'd blathered on so end-
lessly the other day about how he'd never get seriously
involved with another woman, why should she waste her
time with him? She'd said she was off men because of an
unhappy love affair, but what did she know? She was only
twenty-four, for heaven's sake! Hardly out of her teens,
and she probably wanted what most people want eventually—a spouse and children—whether or not she was
willing to admit it.

She stirred, and his arms tightened involuntarily around
her, unwilling to let her go. She surprised him, though,
by just tipping back her head to look at him.

"If you don't mind, I'd rather we ate here," she said
in that husky voice of hers, then once more cradled her
head against his shoulder.

Gray couldn't believe his luck. Nor could he believe
the trust she placed in him. Didn't she know that when a
man was as aroused as he was right now, he couldn't
always be trusted to keep his mind above his belt? It
would be so easy for him to excite her past caring about
the consequences....

He mentally shook himself out of his forbidden musing.
Damn! He didn't like the direction his thoughts were taking. He'd never do a thing like that to any woman, and
certainly not one as innocent as this one seemed to be.

He took her by the shoulders and tenderly put her away
from him. She blinked, as if coming out of a trance.
"Good. I was hoping you'd say that. I've got a freezer
full of dinners. Why don't you come to the kitchen with
me, and we'll select the ones we want to thaw."

He chose fried chicken, she decided on beef Stroganoff;
he tossed a salad, while she fixed hot garlic buttered
French bread. They kept the conversation light, but he felt
self-conscious and could see that she did, too.

Dessert was ice cream and cookies, and afterward Eve cleared the table, while Gray stacked the dishwasher and worried about what was going to happen next. Would Eve insist on leaving right away, or would she stay for the evening? If she stayed, would he be able to carry on an intelligent conversation with her and keep his hands to himself?

Gray started the dishwasher, then turned to Eve. "Do you mind if I switch on the television for a few minutes? It's time for the evening news, and I'd like to catch the weather forecast. See if anything's changed since noon."

She smiled. "By all means, go ahead," she said. "I have to leave anyway—"

He felt as if he'd been punched, even though just moments ago he'd been uneasy about the possibility that she might stay. "No, please, don't! We'll forget all about the weather forecast—"

"That's not it, Gray," she said. "I—I just don't feel it's a good idea for us to spend any more time alone together tonight...."

He had to agree with her on that, but still he couldn't just give in and let her walk away. He needed her in his house, in his arms.

"We can sit clear across the room from each other if you prefer," he offered, but she shook her head.

"I'm sorry, but I really do have to get home. If you still want me to tutor your daughter, I'll be back tomorrow at three. And Gray, I—I'd rather you didn't stay around."

He frowned, but she continued. "I know I said you could, but now I'm afraid it would be too distracting. At least, until we get better acquainted."

Gray nearly choked. How much better acquainted could they get?

Well, he knew the answer to that, and he had to admit that she had a point. It was time to back off again and try to put their relationship into perspective.

Chapter Six

The rest of the week moved along smoothly. At first Tinker was reluctant to even try the assignments Eve had chosen for her, but when Eve got down on the floor with her, and they did the lessons together at Tinker's level, it became more like a game. Tinker actually enjoyed it and was eager to learn.

Eve started her off on first-grade material, even though the child had mastered that pretty well over the years. Eve wanted her to get the feel of success, instead of the constant failure she'd been unable to escape as she'd trailed through second and third grades.

As for Gray, she saw little of him. He would greet her when she arrived, then excuse himself and go to his office at the back of the house, leaving the front rooms for Eve and Tinker to use.

When it was time for her to leave, he was there to thank her and tell her goodbye. He always seemed cheerful but reserved, and she was torn between relief and disappointment. They both knew they couldn't spend much time together without getting intimately involved, but their hormones raged for a touch, a kiss, a night of passion.

On Friday, as Eve was gathering her lesson material together to put in her briefcase, Gray surprised her by coming out of his office a few minutes earlier than usual.

"Tinker," he said, "why don't you go back to the office and watch TV for a few minutes. I want to talk to Ms. Costopoulos."

Eve blinked. Now what? He'd only spoken to her to say hello and goodbye all week, and now he was sending Tinker out of the room so he could talk to her privately. Was he displeased with her tutoring?

Tinker took it in stride. "Okay, Dad. Can I watch *Beauty and the Beast* again?"

Gray grimaced playfully. "Yes, you may, but that tape must be about worn out by now."

"It was, but Grandma and Grandpa sent me a new one for Christmas, remember?" She turned and hurried down the hall.

Eve looked at Gray and smiled. "I gather she's well versed in fairy tales," she said softly.

He didn't comment, but held out his arms. "Come here." His voice quivered and his eyes begged. "I can't wait any longer to hold you. It seems like it's been forever."

She closed her eyes and breathed a little prayer of thanks. He was as eager for her as she was for him! She moved forward and his arms clasped her tightly, while hers fastened around his waist. She tipped her face up to meet his, and his mouth claimed hers, eager and hot.

He tasted her lips, her tongue, her throat, and the sensuous lobes of her ears. Wherever his mouth touched her, it raised her temperature another notch, until she found it almost impossible to remember they were not alone in the house.

With supreme effort, she pushed tentatively against his shoulders. "Gray, don't forget Tinker—"

He moaned quietly. "I won't, sweetheart. I've had over eight years of subconsciously listening for her in the middle of the night, or when she's sick, or getting into mischief. It's become second nature for me now...."

His words trailed off and once again he kissed her, quick and hard. "But you're right," he continued once he'd caught his breath. "This time I came awfully close to getting lost in the sweetness and fire of you."

He hugged her and buried his face in the side of her neck. "Eve," he said raggedly, "spend the weekend with me. It's Bambi's turn to have Tinker. We could go to Deadwood tomorrow, do a little sightseeing, shopping, play a few slot machines. If you haven't seen the Passion Play recently, we could go to Spearfish in the evening and take it in."

What was he suggesting? His agenda was too seductive to fit in with their vows of not letting their association go any further than a teacher-parent relationship. He'd said he wanted to spend the weekend with her, not just the next day. She might be inexperienced, but she wasn't stupid.

He wanted to take her to Deadwood and spend the next two days making love with her in one of those quaint remodeled historic hotels. That's what she wanted, too. Oh, how she wanted it—so bad that she had to clench her jaw to keep from agreeing immediately without a thought to the consequences.

She took a deep breath and prayed for strength. "Oh, Gray, I—that is we..."

He massaged her back lightly. "Honey, we won't do

anything you don't want to. There are no strings attached. I won't pretend that I don't want to spend the night with you, but not if you don't want it, too. I'll bring you home, or we can get separate rooms—"

She put her hand over his mouth and shook her head. "It's not that I don't want to spend the night with you. I want that more than anything. But what became of all our good intentions about not getting intimately involved? It's really a bad idea for a teacher to get entangled in a romantic relationship with the father of one of her pupils. Unless they're engaged to be married. It can get awfully messy."

He kissed the palm that covered his mouth. "It doesn't need to. There's nothing wrong with loving each other. Besides, it's nobody else's business what we're doing, as long as we're discreet and not outraging public decency."

She giggled. "Sounds interesting. Maybe you could explain it to me sometime?"

He bit her neck tenderly. "I'd be even happier to show you," he whispered into her ear.

Delicious as this conversation was, it was getting out of hand. It was time to make a decision. "Why don't we plan to spend tomorrow at Deadwood and see where that takes us?"

She knew that was just a decision to make a decision, and it was risky, as well. It encouraged them both to think they'd be better able to resist temptation when the time came. But Eve knew that thinking about it longer only made it harder to resist, not easier. And it wouldn't make it any less of a mistake if they let their passion overcome their good sense.

He hugged her closer. "That's fine with me. We'll get an early start and stop for breakfast on the way. Okay?"

"Mmm, more than okay," she said, and snuggled into

his embrace for just a minute before pulling away from him. "Now, I really do have to leave." She went back to shoving papers and books into her briefcase. "What time will you pick me up in the morning?"

The following day, Eve was up at the crack of dawn, too excited to sleep any longer. Not because she was eager to see historic Deadwood, the gold-rush town nestled high in a gulch in the Black Hills of South Dakota. She'd been there many times. It was only a short drive from Rapid City, and she'd been going there all her life—sometimes with her parents, sometimes on school trips, and sometimes with friends. She never tired of the exciting view of the "real" Old West as it had been painstakingly reconstructed from an ancient ghost town. But this time she'd be spending the whole day, and maybe more, with Gray, and it wouldn't make any difference where they went as long as they were together.

She dressed warmly in layers: boots, jeans, a T-shirt under a sweatshirt, and a quilted jacket with a colorful knitted stretch hat. It could be pretty chilly up there this time of the year. Deadwood was quite a bit higher than Rapid City: 4,500 feet to Rapid City's 3,200. She could shed some of the outer layers during the day, but it was sure to be cold if they went to Spearfish to see the Passion Play, the Christian dramatization of the reenactment of the crucifixion and resurrection of Jesus of Nazareth. That was an outdoor evening event, and the temperature was always frigid.

As she was packing her backpack, it occurred to her that she might want her toothbrush, and obviously it was of little use without toothpaste. She dropped the two articles in the bag and was starting to zip it closed when she thought of her makeup. She had a tube of lipstick in her jacket pocket, but they'd be gone all day, and she'd no doubt want to touch up her powder, blusher and mascara at times.

While she gathered up those items, she remembered her brush and comb. It wouldn't hurt to take her curling iron and blow-dryer too, and what about a change of underwear—

That thought finally registered, and she cut it off with a mortified gasp. Without even realizing it, she was packing for an overnight trip.

Abashed, she picked up the canvas bag and started to turn it over to empty it out, then stopped. Oh, what the hell. There wasn't a thing in there that she might not need for a one-day excursion, and even if there was, Gray wouldn't know it. She wasn't going to repack.

Gray picked her up at her apartment right on time, and started the day off joyfully with a lingering kiss. He, too, was dressed warmly and in Western-style clothes, complete with the Stetson hat.

Eve chuckled and touched the wide brim. "Hey, what happened to the TV reporter I made a date with? Looks like I got a cowboy, instead. All that's missing are the guns."

His blue eyes twinkled. "All men are cowboys in Deadwood, sweetheart, and it looks like that schoolmarm I asked to accompany me turned out to be a cowgirl." He held her away from him and looked her over. "What's more, there's not a thing missing from her."

They both laughed, and within a few minutes were in the Jaguar and on their way. They drove as far as a truck stop, on the outskirts of Rapid City, famous for its man-size breakfasts and finally rolled into Deadwood around ten o'clock.

"Okay, Luv, what do you want to do first?" he asked as he parked the car. "The casinos are up and running, the shops are open and waiting for us to come and spend our money, and there are always several gold mine tours that run every so often during the day."

Eve stepped out of the car and stretched. "Well, why don't we be really decadent and start off the day at the slot machines. I've got a twenty-dollar bill hidden in my wallet. That's my gambling money. When it's gone, I'll quit and go on to something else."

He got out of the car, too, and came around to meet her at the front. "Sure, you will," he teased, "and it never rains unless I forecast that it will."

She looked up at him. "You don't think I can do it?"

They started to walk. "I'm sure you think you can, but twenty one-dollar tokens will be gone before you even get warmed up."

"I don't play with dollars," she explained. "I play the nickel machines only."

He gave her an odd look, somewhere between disbelief and astonishment. "You're almost too good to be true, do you know that?"

She was uncomfortable with such high praise. "Oh, come on, Gray," she said lightly. "I work hard for my money. I'm not going to just throw it away. Twenty dollars isn't too much to spend for entertainment, especially since I don't get up here often. But anything over that is a foolish risk that I can't afford. Please don't think I've sprouted wings just because I try to keep my finances under control."

Gray put his arm around her waist and clasped her to his side as they walked. "Okay, I won't look for wings on you if you don't expect horns to germinate out of my head—because I'm going to play with dollars instead of dimes.''

''Deal,'' she said happily as they turned into the lobby of the Midnight Star casino where all of movie star Kevin Costner's costumes were displayed.

True to her word, Eve quit gambling when the last of her twenty dollars was gone. Gray, against her protest, stopped then, too, even though he was still ahead.

''I didn't bring you here just to gamble,'' he said as he cashed in his winnings. ''I want us to do whatever pleases you. So what's next on the agenda?''

They spent the rest of the day bouncing from one activity to another. They toured the Broken Boot mine and learned how a real gold mine operated in the Old West; exclaimed over the '76 Museum with the largest collection of authentic horse-drawn vehicles that brought supplies and settlers to the gold camps; browsed the rustic boutiques; and climbed Boot Hill to view the graves of Wild Bill Hickok, Calamity Jane, Preacher Smith, Potato Creek Johnny, and other long-ago legendary figures.

However, the most breathtaking sight of all was the panoramic view of Deadwood at sunset.

By then it was dinnertime, and Gray suggested they eat in the renovated dining area of the historic Franklin Hotel. That reminded Eve that she was going to have to make a decision soon about spending the night here—with him.

That quandary had been in the back of her mind all day, but she kept pushing it away, unwilling to deal with it until later.

Well, ''later'' had caught up with her, and she couldn't put her decision off much longer. They were going to have to make plans one way or the other. She wanted Gray so much, but she didn't want to be his ''significant other.'' On the other hand, that's all he was offering now, or ever would offer.

They settled on the Franklin Hotel restaurant, which was known to feature the best steak in this vast cattle country. They were waiting for their dessert to be served, when Gray put his hand over Eve's on the table. ''Have you made up your mind yet about what you want to do this evening? We can take in the reenactment in the old town hall of the trial of Jack McCall for the murder of Wild Bill Hickok, drive to Spearfish and see the Passion Play, or...''

He hesitated, and she sensed that he wasn't going to pressure her to spend the night with him. It was all up to her now.

She took a deep breath, and hoped she wasn't about to make the biggest mistake of her life. ''I prefer the 'or,' if you don't mind.''

His face lit up and he squeezed her hand. ''Mind? You've just made me the happiest man on earth.''

He raised her hand to his mouth and kissed it, just as the waiter arrived with their blueberry pie.

It seemed to Gray that it took forever for them to finish eating, register at the hotel, and be shown to their room. But once the door closed behind them, he took Eve in his arms and did what he'd been dying to do all day: he kissed her, passionately.

At first she seemed somewhat restrained in her response, and he tried to take it easy and hold back a little. After all, they had the entire night, and he had to admit it bothered him that she obviously wasn't very experienced at this. Was it possible that she was a virgin?

No, he couldn't believe that. She was twenty-four years old and had graduated from college. Also, she'd mentioned something about having a relationship at one time that didn't work out.

He nuzzled the sensitive hollows on either side of her neck and felt her heartbeat speed up. She tipped back her head, making it easier for him to feather kisses across her smooth, graceful throat. He could actually feel the little purring sounds she was making.

They pushed each other's jackets off their shoulders and let them fall to the floor. Then he pulled her sweatshirt over her head and tossed it aside, only to discover that she had on a T-shirt under that.

His hands ached for the touch of her bare flesh, but her fingers fumbling with the pearl snaps on his flannel shirt were almost as erotic. It took all his patience to stand still and let her take her time, instead of ripping the snaps apart.

It wasn't until she got the blasted thing open that he was reminded that he had also worn a T-shirt under it. They looked at each other for a brief moment, then broke out into laughter.

"I suggest we get out of our boots, at least," he teased. "Things could get a little uncomfortable if we don't."

He hoped a bit of humor would keep him from going up in flames, or rushing her.

"I'll go along with that," she said, and sat down on the side of the bed.

Gray hunkered down in front of her and pulled off first one of her boots, then the other.

"Now it's my turn," she insisted, and stood.

He put his arms around her and drew her close. "If that's what you want," he murmured into her hair, and ran his fingers down her spine.

He felt her shiver and knew she was as excited as he. He was overwhelmingly tempted to lay her down on the

bed and take her right then and there, boots and all, but
the very fact of that temptation made him determined not
to give in to it.

He shouldn't be doing this at all, he thought. She was
so young and inexperienced compared to him. The least
he could do was take his time and make it as memorable
for her as he could. She'd apparently had at least one lover
who was less than satisfactory.

"Gray, I can't take your boots off if you don't sit
down," she teased him playfully, and all his hesitation
evaporated.

"Oh, Eve, I want you," he groaned. He cupped her
derriere and lifted her enough to rub his groin into hers,
to relieve some of the pressure in his swollen manhood.
She uttered a sharp little cry, and surprised him by locking
her knees against his hips and pushing even closer to him,
throwing him off balance.

They tumbled onto the bed and started groping at the
clothes each of them still wore. He tugged at her T-shirt,
trying to get it out from under her tight-fitting jeans. She
had her hand between their entwined bodies, fumbling for
the snaps on their zippers—and nearly driving him over
the edge.

He'd been vaguely aware of a noise in the background,
but paid no attention until he heard a man's voice calling
his name, quietly at first but more loudly each time it was
uttered.

"Mr. Flint, please open the door! I have an urgent message for you! Mr. Flint, I must talk to you!"

Gray was enraged. What a time to be interrupted! Besides, nobody knew he was here.

By now, Eve had heard it, too. She tried to sit up, but
he held her down. He couldn't let her go—not now.

"Just lie still and keep quiet, sweetheart," he whispered. "Whoever it is will give up and go away."

"No, you must answer it," she insisted. "He'll have the whole hotel roused if this goes on much longer. Who is it?"

"I don't have any idea," he growled. "I didn't tell a soul we were coming up here. Did you?"

"No, nobody."

The knocking and calling came again. Gray swore as he stood up and rearranged his clothes, then headed for the door.

"Who are you, and what do you want?" he called before turning the lock.

"Highway Patrol, Mr. Flint," came the voice from the other side. "Would you please open the door? I have a message for you."

Highway Patrol? What did they want with him? And how did they know where to find him?

He glanced over his shoulder to make sure Eve was decently covered. She was sitting on the edge of the bed, bootless and endearingly tousled, but otherwise proper, So he grudgingly opened the door to confront a uniformed peace officer.

"Well?" he barked, not giving an inch.

The officer looked embarrassed. "Sorry to disturb you, sir, but you are Grayson Flint, the weatherman on TV, aren't you?"

Gray's anger was slowly changing to anxiety. This was no case of mistaken identity. The officer had the man he was looking for. But why was he looking for him?

"Yes, I'm Grayson Flint," he admitted, a little less belligerently this time. "What do you want? And how did you find me here?"

"Sorry, sir, but do you mind if I come in? There are people out here in the hall eager to know what's going on that merits all the racket."

Gray was caught in an uncomfortable dilemma. He didn't want Eve exposed as his overnight guest, but neither was he willing to discuss whatever it was that brought the police to his and Eve's hotel room in front of a hall full of curious onlookers.

Fortunately, the decision was taken out of his hands by Eve herself. "By all means come in, Officer," she said from where she sat on the bed. "If you'd like, I can go down to the lobby—"

"No way," Gray interrupted. "I don't know what's going on, but I haven't done anything you can't know about."

He stepped back to allow the officer to enter, then shut the door. The other man took off his cap and twisted it nervously. "We've been looking for you for almost an hour, Mr. Flint. I've been told to tell you to call your wife. It's urgent."

Gray blinked. What was going on, anyway? Had some of the guys at the TV station found out he and Eve were coming here today, and decided to play one of those stupid, embarrassing typically male pranks on him?

"I'm afraid you're being used, Officer. I don't have a wife, but I do have some pretty raunchy pals at the TV station who aren't above pulling a stunt like this—"

"I suggest you investigate, sir," he said as he reached into his breast pocket, pulled out a folded piece of paper and handed it to Gray. "The caller identified herself as Mrs. Bambi Flint, and said she was calling from the hospital at Rapid City. There's been an accident—"

Shock immobilized Gray for a moment. "Bambi! Has something happened to Tinker?"

He heard Eve gasp, and then felt her comforting hand on his shoulder. But he was too stunned to respond to her.

"Bambi Flint is my *ex*-wife, Officer. Did she say anything about our daughter, Tinker? Is she ill or injured?"

The other man shook his head. "I don't know. I didn't take the call when it came in, and all the dispatcher told me was that the woman sounded pretty hysterical. She asked us to find you and tell you to call her immediately at the number written on the paper."

Gray didn't even respond, but strode across the room and dialed the number on the old-fashioned telephone that matched the other furnishings. As he listened to the ring at the other end, he heard Eve and the officer talking quietly in the background.

Finally he heard someone pick up the phone at the other end. "This is Grayson Flint," he said tersely. "I understand my ex-wife and daughter have been brought there following an accident. Can you tell me how they are?"

The woman's voice answered. "Names, please."

"Bernice and Sarah Flint, but they may be registered as Bambi and Tinker. Sarah, known as Tinker, is the child."

There was a long pause while the woman checked her files, and Gray paced nervously in the restricted space allowed by the phone cord. "Mr. Flint, Mrs. Flint has only cuts and bruises. The child is still being treated, and I have no information on her yet, but Mrs. Flint has asked us to let her talk to you as soon as you call."

"All right, fine, put her on."

There was another wait while he paced some more, then finally Bambi spoke. "Gray! Oh, Gray, please come. I need you." She did sound hysterical.

"Bambi, what happened?" he demanded. "What kind of accident was it, and how is Tinker? Is she badly hurt?"

"I think so," Bambi sobbed. "She was all bloody, and

crying…they brought both of us here in an ambulance… The paramedics were working on her…"

Bambi sniffled. "Oh, darling, where are you? I couldn't find you… I tried every place I could think of…. Please, come quickly. They won't let me be with her in the examining room. I need you so—"

"I'm leaving immediately," he said shortly. "Has Jim been notified? Is he with her now?" He trusted Jim—Dr. James Whitney—Tinker's pediatrician and Gray's golfing partner.

"I don't know. I haven't seen him, but I can ask."

"Never mind, I don't want to waste any more time. I'll be there in about an hour."

He broke off the connection, then turned to Eve. "Tinker's been injured in an accident. I don't know what kind or how badly, but we have to leave right away."

"Of course," Eve said, and he saw the shock and pain in her expressive eyes as he shifted his gaze to the officer.

"Thanks, Officer," Gray said, and put out his hand. "I appreciate your hunting me down."

The officer took the proffered hand. "That's my job. I just hope your little girl's all right."

Eve cringed in the seat beside Gray as he raced the little Jaguar with the big engine down the mountainside. She knew that he was a good driver, and she could certainly understand his urgent need to get to the hospital and find out how badly his daughter was injured, but still, the speed at which he was traveling was dangerous.

She had an urgent need, too: the need to comfort him and assure him everything was all right. But she couldn't. She didn't know any more about what had happened than he did. She'd taken the opportunity to question the highway patrol officer while Gray was talking to Bambi, but he didn't have much information, either.

"I just don't understand what could have happened," Gray said while he concentrated on the road ahead of him. "It was probably a car accident, but I never found out for sure."

Thank heavens that was one question Eve could assure him of. She put her hand on his thigh. "It was an automobile accident. I asked the officer, and he said, according to their report, it was a one-vehicle collision—but that's all he knew."

Gray groaned. "I knew something like that was going to happen someday. Bambi drives like a bat out of hell. I've threatened several times to have her license taken away from her, but she always promised to be more careful."

Speaking of a bat out of hell, Eve was tempted to point out that that was the way *he* was driving now, but she restrained herself.

Instead, she ran her fingertips over his thigh. Not enough to take his mind off his driving, but hopefully enough to relax him a little.

It did the trick. He let up a fraction on the gas, and put his hand over hers. "Did that officer tell you how the highway patrol knew we were in Deadwood? I was careful not to tell anybody where we were going because I didn't want us to be disturbed. I didn't even bring my cell phone."

"Neither did I." Eve admitted. "But somehow Bambi knew we were there. Apparently she called the highway patrol and told them you were in Deadwood and that there'd been an emergency at home. She needed to get in touch with you. She gave them your car make and license, and all they had to do was look for it, which, in case you hadn't noticed, is easy. It sticks out like a red flag.''

He grunted and put his hand back on the steering wheel as they continued to hurtle down the road.

At the outskirts of Rapid City, Gray finally slowed down somewhat. Even so, the tires squealed and both of them were thrown forward—though restrained by seatbelts—when Gray slammed on the brakes in front of the hospital.

Without a word he opened his door, leaped out of the car, and ran through the wide double doors into the emergency room. Eve wasn't far behind him. Not far enough to miss the sight of Bambi running toward him, blood stains on her clothes, tears streaming down her face.

"Gray! Oh, darling, I thought you'd never get here!" She threw herself into his arms, and he clasped her against him and held her.

Eve felt sick. Dear, sweet Tinker. That precious child who would never harm anybody. Was she...?

No. She wouldn't even let herself think of such a monstrous happening.

At least Gray and Bambi had each other to lean on. It was natural that each would seek comfort from the other at a time like this.

Bambi had had it right all along. They were still husband and wife, in all the ways that counted.

Chapter Seven

Eve shrank back, not wanting to be seen by either Gray or Bambi as they embraced. The Flint family didn't need her intruding on their private grief. There was a large potted plant near the door that she could stand behind without being noticed. Especially by a mother and father as intent on their own tragedy as Bambi and Gray were.

Neither could she hear them, and she longed for word of Tinker. How was she? Were her injuries serious? Life threatening? That sweet little girl! She was so young. So vital.

Eve finally saw Gray break away from Bambi and go over to the admission desk, then cross the room to one of the curtained areas. Was that where Tinker was? It must be, but what condition was she in?

Once Gray disappeared behind the curtain, Bambi opened her purse, took out a package of cigarettes and, with a glance at the No Smoking sign, pushed open one of the large swinging glass doors and went outside.

Eve took the opportunity to hurry over to the desk to

ask about Tinker. She identified herself as the child's tutor and a friend of the family.

"She has a head injury, but it doesn't seem to be serious," the woman at the desk told her. "They'll probably keep her overnight for observation, though."

Eve felt light-headed with relief, and tears welled in her eyes.

Now she had just one more request. "Do you have a notepad I can write on?"

The woman reached under the counter and handed her one. Eve wrote a quick note, folded it over, put Gray's name on it, and asked the woman to give it to him when he was through talking to the doctor.

Gray didn't need to be saddled with her tonight. She went out the front door, hailed a cab and asked the driver to take her home.

Eve had been home about an hour and a half—long enough to shower and get into the pullover cotton-knit sleep shirt and boxer shorts she liked to sleep in—when there was a knock at the door. A glance at her watch told her it was almost midnight. Although she assumed it was Gray, as a precaution she turned on the porch light and looked through the peephole.

She was right. He was standing out there, slumped and looking incredibly weary. She'd hoped he would call her after he read her note telling him she was taking a cab home, but she hadn't expected him to come over.

She opened the door, and he stepped inside and took her in his arms. "I'm sorry I left you on your own back at the hospital." His voice was filled with remorse. "By the time I made sure Tinker was all right, got all the consents given and papers signed, and saw her settled in her room in the pediatric ward, you were gone."

"Don't think another thing about it. I'd have been disappointed in you if she hadn't been your first priority." She snuggled into his embrace. "How is Tinker?"

"As far as they can tell, she'll be all right," he said. "But she's had a head injury, so they're keeping her in the hospital until her pediatrician examines her tomorrow."

She raised her head and studied him. He still looked ghastly, although now the lines of anxiety were gone. "That's what the lady at the desk told me when I inquired about her before I left." She hesitated a moment, then asked, "And how's Bambi? I was careful not to let her see me."

He sighed. "That's probably just as well. I don't need her throwing it up to me that I was out of town with you when our daughter was injured."

Eve knew he hadn't meant that to sound as if he'd been cheating on his wife when he took Eve to Deadwood, but it did. And it slashed at her like a whip. Bambi had a way of making Eve feel like the other woman in an otherwise happy marriage, and Eve found that untenable.

Probably because she'd been made to feel guilty, too, her first inclination was to fight back. "Oh? And just whose fault was it that her daughter was hurt? What happened?"

Gray relaxed his hold on her and turned them in the direction of the sofa. "Do you mind if we sit down? I'm about out on my feet."

She silently scolded herself for being so unobservant, and walked to the couch with him. He took off his jacket and tossed it across a nearby chair before they settled themselves in a comfortable embrace in the corner of the richly upholstered sofa.

Eve knew she shouldn't allow this. After what happened today, she had a lot more thinking to do before she let herself get caught up in a love affair with this man. It was just as well something had interrupted them earlier this evening. Not that she would have wished for poor little Tinker to be hurt, but it was that incident that had brought her out of her romantic reverie and made her face a few hard truths.

Gray's hand fondled her bare thigh, then found its way under her nightshirt and cupped her unencumbered breast, not urgently but gently, as if searching for warmth. It was only then that she remembered what she was wearing. The nightclothes were an obvious invitation, and that was not the message she wanted to send. She knew that if he drew her into the sweet delirium of foreplay, she wouldn't have the strength to stop him.

"I—I'd better go get dressed," she said, and tried to sit up. But he held her back.

"No, please, don't," he begged. "I'm not trying to seduce you. Frankly, I doubt if I could...uh...perform right now. I just need you with me. I need your compassion, your warmth. I like the silky smoothness of your bare legs and the softness of your beautiful breasts."

How could she resist him when he talked like that? She lay back against him and let herself enjoy. What would a little innocent making-out hurt? These stolen moments of bliss could bring them so much pleasure....

Those were her last thoughts until she woke wrapped in Gray's arms on the wide sofa, sun streaming in the windows.

Daylight! They'd slept all night and now it was—she held up her arm and looked at her watch—six o'clock! Gray had missed his first two weather forecasts, and was about to miss the third—

She started to struggle out of the iron grip he had on

her, but then remembered. It was Sunday. Gray didn't work on Sundays.

She relaxed and nestled against him. She'd never before fallen asleep while necking with a man. She wondered which one of them conked out first. The last she remembered, they were sitting up. When did they lie down?

He stirred, and she raised her head and looked right into his blue eyes. They registered the same shock she knew hers did. "Eve? What are you doing here?"

She smiled. "I live here, sweetheart. What about you?"

He raised up on his elbow and looked around. "Holy Moses." He grunted. "I've never in my whole life slept so soundly. What did we...? I mean, when did we—?" he sputtered. "Oh, hell," he said, and shifted around to sit up at the end of the couch with his feet on the floor. "What did I do to you?"

She could see that he was really upset, and she put her hand on his arm. "I don't remember going to sleep, either, but I do know that you didn't do a thing to me, Gray. We were both worn out and couldn't stay awake. I only woke up a few minutes before you did."

He put his hand over hers and smiled. "Well, I'm glad to hear that. The first time we make love, I want us both wide awake and participating."

He frowned. "On the other hand, if you're telling me that I spent the night with you and actually slept, I'd better start worrying about my virility. I really am getting old."

She laughed, but the twinkle in his eyes suddenly turned to alarm. "Oh, God, I've got to call the hospital," he said, and jumped up. "When I left, I told the nurse in charge to call me at home in case they wanted to reach me."

"There's a phone in the kitchen," she directed him. "Meanwhile I'll get dressed."

She brushed her teeth and splashed cool water on her face in the bathroom, then went to the bedroom and quickly got into a navy-blue pants suit with a coordinated red-white-and-blue striped knit shirt.

Gray was still on the phone when she came out of the bedroom, and his eyes widened in appreciation as he continued his telephone conversation. "Okay, then," he was saying. "I'll be over in a few minutes. If Dr. Whitney gets there before I do, ask him not to leave until I see him."

He hung up the phone and turned to Eve. "Wow! If all lady sailors looked like you, the young men in this country would be queuing up around the block to enlist."

He put both arms around her and kissed her, long and hungrily.

"The hospital told me Tinker had a restful night and is still asleep," he told Eve when they finally broke apart. "I need to talk to her pediatrician, but they're not expecting him to put in an appearance for about an hour. That will give me time to stop at the house and shower, shave and change clothes. You will come with me, won't you?"

"Just try and stop me," she said, then hesitated. "That is, if it won't cause trouble with Bambi."

He scowled. "Bambi will be lucky if I don't press charges against her, and she knows it. She was driving recklessly and didn't have Tinker belted in. I don't think she'll give us any problems."

Eve blinked. "What do you mean 'driving recklessly'?"

"Last night after you left the hospital, I caught up with one of the police officers who was investigating the accident," Gray explained. "He told me Bambi was speeding, took a curve too fast, lost control of the car, and slammed into a tree. The car was totaled. She was able to brace herself by holding on to the steering wheel, but Tinker was thrown around and hit her head against the windshield.''

Eve shivered. How could a mother be so careless as to put her own child in danger? It made her wonder how fit the woman was to have even part-time custody of Tinker.

An hour later, Gray and Eve entered the hospital, inquired about Tinker at the information desk, and were directed to the pediatric wing on the third floor. Gray had cleaned up and was now wearing tan slacks, a brown print shirt and a tan V-neck pullover. He looked every inch the TV personality, and heads turned in recognition as Gray and Eve threaded their way up and down the halls of the hospital.

There were two beds in Tinker's room; she was in the one closest to the window. The top of her bed was partially upright, and she was reclining, a tray table containing her breakfast across her lap.

Eve gasped and bit her lip to keep from crying out. Besides the bandage on her head, Tinker had two black eyes and numerous other visible cuts and bruises.

"Daddy!" she yelped, and dropped her spoon into a bowl of hot cereal as she raised her arms to him. "I want to go home!"

Eve felt him stiffen beside her, and knew he was shocked, too. Apparently she hadn't looked this bad last night.

Quickly Gray walked to the bed, leaned down and hugged her, trying not to knock over anything on the tray. "I know you do, baby, but we'll have to see what Dr. Jim has to say."

He kissed her lightly on her bandage, then straightened up. "Meanwhile, look who I brought to see you."

He motioned to Eve, who was still standing at the doorway. She walked into the room. "Good morning, Tinker. I hope you're feeling better this morning."

"Eve!" she said, using Eve's first name for the first time. Again she held out her arms for a hug.

Eve hurried over and obliged, then sat down on the opposite side of the bed from Gray. She'd never known Tinker to show so much affection before, and it delighted her to be a recipient.

"My head hurts," she said unhappily in answer to Eve's comment. "And I threw up three times last night."

She looked around the room, careful not to move her head too much. "Where's Mom? Did she get hurt in the accident, too?"

"Just some sore ribs and a few scrapes and bruises," Gray said. "Don't you remember? She and I were both here last night when they brought you up to this room. We stayed with you until you went to sleep, and then I took Mom home. Her car won't run. It had to be towed away."

This was news to Eve. Gray hadn't said anything to her about taking Bambi home.

"Don't be too mad at Mom," Tinker said to Gray. "I gave her a bad time about wearing the seatbelt." Tinker looked down. "She said you'd be mad at her if she didn't make me buckle it, but I talked her out of it."

Tears pooled in the little girl's eyes. "I—I'm glad she wasn't hurt, too."

Gray moved the tray table away, sat down on his side of the bed, and took her in his arms. "Don't you worry about anything, sweetheart," he murmured. "Mom's all right, and I'm going to take you home as soon as Dr. Jim says I can—''

"Is someone taking my name in vain?"

All three of them looked up to see a good-looking man, about the same age as Gray, entering the room wearing a white lab coat and followed by a nurse.

Gray released Tinker and stood. "Well, it's about time you got here," he growled with a big smile that belied his tone. "I was beginning to think I was going to have to send out for another pediatrician."

"No way!" This time the doctor's voice was serious. "I've already had harsh words with my answering service for not calling me when my favorite little patient here was brought into the ER." He winked at Tinker, and she giggled.

Again he turned his attention to Gray. "I was in town, but Winnie and I celebrated our tenth anniversary yesterday, so we left the kids with Winnie's parents and rented the VIP suite at the Hilton hotel. Trying to find a little privacy, you know?"

Gray laughed. "You don't need to spell it out—I know exactly what you mean. I was out of town when Bambi was trying to get hold of me. But Tinker was well taken care of."

The doctor nodded. "Yeah, Leonard Thompson is an excellent physician—but Tinker's special."

"Oh, and speaking of special ladies," Gray said, turning to Eve, "I'd like you to meet my friend Eve Costopoulos. She's a teacher who is tutoring Tinker this summer. She's also almost singlehandedly trying to raise enough funds to put a new roof on the building where she teaches. Eve, this is Tinker's pediatrician and my favorite golfing partner, Dr. Jim Whitney."

After Eve and Jim greeted each other, Jim said, "Now

I'm going to ask you two to wait in the little waiting room at the end of the hall while I examine Tinker. It won't take long, and then I'll join you, and we can talk.''

They found the small, comfortably furnished room complete with a telephone and two vending machines, one for coffee and one for sweet rolls.

"Do you want some coffee?" Gray asked.

Eve remembered that they hadn't had anything to eat yet this morning, and realized she was hungry. "Yes, please. Black, and also one of those cinnamon rolls."

In less than half an hour, the doctor appeared with the happy news that although Tinker was badly bruised and would probably have stiff muscles and a headache for a while, she didn't appear to be seriously injured.

That didn't satisfy Gray. "How can you say she's not seriously injured when she looks like someone's pummeled her? I was shocked when I saw her this morning. She looked bad enough last night, but—"

"Now, calm down," Jim said. "I didn't mean her injuries aren't serious, just that they're not life-threatening. She wants to go home, and I know you want to take her home. But I'd like to keep her here for another twenty-four hours, just to make sure. Head injuries can be tricky things, especially in a child, and she can be more thoroughly monitored here."

Gray nodded. "Whatever you think best, Jim. I just hope she won't be too upset about it."

"You and Bambi are welcome to stay with her," Jim suggested. "I understand Bambi was also examined last night, but was only shaken up and had some ribs bruised."

"I'll deal with her," Gray said through his teeth. "In fact, I'm going to do that right now, as soon as I reassure Tinker and get her settled down."

Eve saw Jim frown, and she felt apprehensive, too. "Don't you think you'd better wait until you've calmed down a little before you confront Bambi?" Jim asked. "She didn't smash that car into the tree on purpose."

"She might as well have," Gray said grimly. "I can't count the number of times I've paid her speeding tickets and lectured her on safe driving. I even made her take a course in driving safety, but the whole thing goes in one ear and out the other."

He drew in a deep breath, then exhaled. "At least now she doesn't have a car. Maybe having to walk every place she goes will grab her attention."

After Gray had convinced Tinker that spending another day and night in the hospital wouldn't be so bad, he drove to Eve's apartment complex. When he shut off the engine, she turned to him, and he took her in his arms—difficult though that was with the gear shift between them. And they savored a warm moist kiss that almost made him forget why he was leaving her here alone instead of coming in with her.

"Are you sure you don't want to come with me?" he asked, even though he knew what the answer would be.

She rubbed her cheek against his. "No, Gray, I can't. This is a family problem, and I'm not part of the family. My presence would just make it sticky for all of us."

He knew that Eve was right, he thought as he drove on to Bambi's house. He was going to raise havoc with Bambi for her carelessness with their child, and it was a private matter. Nevertheless, he hated to let Eve go. He realized that he needed her moral and emotional support. Tangling with Bambi was always a frustrating and maddening experience.

God knows, he'd been patient with her up until now.

Too patient. She'd been the only child of adoring parents who'd not only nourished her inborn childish personality, but encouraged it by caving in to her every wish.

Still, he couldn't place all the blame on her parents. He'd been at fault, too. Too often, rather than taking the time and effort to try to teach her, he'd given in and let her have her own way. Unfortunately, he'd never been able to convey to her what was acceptable in a relationship, and what wasn't. Also, he'd found it easier to smooth things over rather than make her accept the consequences of her immaturity.

Bambi simply wouldn't understand that she couldn't have everything she wanted, and have it now.

He parked the car at the curb in front of Bambi's house and walked up to the door, all the while telling himself to calm down and think before he spoke. It was imperative that he get his message across, and he wouldn't accomplish that by yelling at her.

He knew it would take drastic measures to convince her that he was no longer going to be coerced by apologies, tears or appeals to his love for their daughter.

He'd tried hard to be fair in the matter of Tinker's custody, but after what happened yesterday, she was going to have to prove to him that she was willing to accept the responsibility that went with it.

Chapter Eight

Eve's phone rang at about six o'clock, and much to her delight it was Gray. "I need to talk to you. Any chance you could have supper with me?"

His tone was brusque and somewhat impersonal.

"Y-Yes, of course, I'll be happy to," she stammered. "Gray, is something wrong? Is Tinker all right? Is Bambi going to make things difficult?"

"Nothing's really wrong, honey," he hurried to assure her. "I just want to talk to you, tell you about my conversation with Bambi, but most of all I want to be with you."

Her misgivings drained away. "I want that, too," she said in a near whisper. "Where do you want me to meet you?"

He didn't hesitate. "Your apartment, as soon as I can get there. I'll bring food, you just bring yourself. Okay?"

Eve smiled. "Okay, don't keep me waiting."

"There's not a hailstorm's chance in Hades of that," he muttered. "See ya!"

* * *

Gray arrived on time, with his arms full of white carryout food sacks. She'd been delighted at the thought of seeing him again, but she was also curious and uneasy. What had happened during his showdown with Bambi?

"You're feeling hunger pangs?" she teased as she eyed the numerous containers.

"And hello to you, too," he said with a grin, and gave her a quick kiss. A kiss that warmed her heart. "I got Chinese, but I didn't know which dishes you preferred, so I ordered a little of everything. I figured you could keep what's left over and warm it up for the next few days."

"Sounds good," she said enthusiastically. "I like anything Asian. Just put everything on the counter in the kitchen, and I'll dish it up. We'd better eat before it gets cold."

He headed for the small kitchen. "I was afraid you were going to say that," he grumbled in a melodramatic tone of voice.

"Did you have something better in mind for us to do?" she teased.

"Damn straight!" he said. He put the sacks on the counter, then turned and encircled her waist with his arms.

"Kiss me," he whispered, and lowered his face to meet her upturned one. Her lips parted beneath his, and he rimmed them with his tongue. She opened to him, and he invaded her with a passionate intimacy that made her shiver.

Reluctantly, he raised his head and pressed her face into his chest. "I've waited too long for that," he murmured against her hair. "But much as I'd like to continue this I'm not going to—"

His voice broke and he kissed the top of her head, then

released her. "At least not now. I didn't come here to rush you into bed, although the temptation is almost overwhelming. There's something you have to know before this relationship goes any further. We can talk while we eat."

Eve was confused. It seemed as if all they ever did was get each other all heated up and then break it off to talk.

She'd set the table for two and put the containers of food out. Once they'd served themselves, Gray told her about his confrontation that morning with Bambi. Gray had lectured Bambi about not buckling up Tinker in the car, but Bambi had made light of the accident. Gray was forced to tell Bambi he was going to find out if he had grounds to petition the court for custody of Tinker.

Eve listened, glad to hear that he was finally laying down the law to his ex-wife, and appalled that Bambi could be so blasé about her small daughter's welfare. Was it possible that she really didn't understand the danger to which she'd subjected Tinker?

"So, I met with my lawyer, Aaron Fox, and he's going to see Bambi tomorrow," Gray concluded as he drained his tea cup.

Eve picked at her egg roll. "Are you really going to petition for physical custody?" she asked. "You told me once before that you'd threatened her with that, but that you didn't really want to do it."

He sighed. "I still don't, but Tinker's safety comes before any other consideration. Bambi's dependence on me is annoying, but I can put up with it as long as I feel she's doing a good job of looking after Tinker. That is no longer the case."

Gray looked and sounded tired and discouraged. He was a kind man, and Eve could see that he didn't relish playing the role of the heartless father trying to take a child away from her mother.

She reached across the small space of table between them and put her hand on his. "If you think there's any danger to Tinker then you have no choice but to bring it to the attention of the court. What does your lawyer say?"

Gray turned his hand over and clasped hers. "Pretty much the same thing you just did, but he warned me that taking her away from her mother won't be easy if Bambi fights it. That auto accident by itself isn't really very strong evidence. It was a first-time offense—except for her speeding tickets—and unless we can prove recklessness, a car accident could have happened to anybody. That's why I'm hoping we can impress Bambi enough by talking tough to get her to shape up and let me have Tinker without a battle."

Gray shook his head. "I've told Aaron what I want if we do have to go to court. That includes physical custody, a reduction in child support payments, and no alimony. That means she'll have to go to work full time. Aaron is going to spell it all out to her. There's no other way. She won't listen to me."

Eve retrieved her hand and took a sip of her tea. "And what if she agrees to take better care of Tinker? Can you trust her to keep her word?"

He sighed. "Probably not, but she'll always have the threat of legal action hanging over her. That might keep her in line. She's already lost some of the spousal support, as Aaron will tell her. That wasn't mandated by the court. I've been paying it on my own so she could stay home and take care of our daughter. I'm afraid that left her too much time to meddle in my affairs. But now Tinker spends most of the day in school during the school year, and is old enough to have a baby-sitter in the summer."

"But will you be able to find a baby-sitter who'll work from four-thirty to seven-thirty in the morning?" Eve asked skeptically.

Gray shrugged. "I doubt it. Possibly a college girl or an older woman who suffers from insomnia, but I hope it won't come to that. I don't want Tinker caught in the middle of a battle between her mother and father. That's why I've pretty much given in to Bambi over these past three years."

Eve could sympathize with the bind he was in, and wished there was something she could do to help, but when she tried, all she did was make it worse.

"You said you were going to take Tinker home with you when she's released from the hospital," Eve reminded him. "Will you be able to find a sitter on such short notice?"

"I have a cousin who works the night shift at a café here in town," he said. "She's agreed to come over to the house when she gets off work and spend the rest of the night and morning there. That won't be for long, though, because she's moving to Sioux Falls in a couple of weeks. But it will give me time to find permanent help."

"Do you think Bambi will be able to get a job?" Eve asked.

Gray leaned foreword with his elbows on the table, and rubbed the back of his neck as if trying to iron out some kinks. "I don't see why not. She's a great restaurant hostess. She'll be first in line to take it over full time when there's an opening. Meanwhile, she has a small inheritance from her mother that is invested in stocks and bonds. It will keep her solvent for a while if necessary."

He looked so uncomfortable as he probed at his nape

that Eve couldn't stand it any longer. She got up and walked around the table to stand behind him. "Let me help," she said as she gently disentangled his hands and replaced them with her own.

Leaning down, she rubbed her cheek against his temple. "Just relax," she whispered in his ear, and gently kneaded her fingers into the taut muscles of his neck and shoulders. "You're all tied up in knots."

"Oooh, that feels good," he said. It was more of a sigh than a statement, as she dug her fingers deeper into his aching shoulders.

"Lean back," she coaxed, and put her hands under his chin to guide his head to rest in the valley between her breasts. Then she resumed massaging the muscles on both sides of his spine.

He sank into her softness with a tremor. "Sweetheart, if you're trying to relax me, I gotta tell you, this is not the way to go about it."

She kissed the top of his head. "Oh, I don't know," she teased. "You seem pretty relaxed to me."

He rubbed his cheek against her arm. "But not for long, I guarantee you."

"It must have been sleeping all night scrunched up on the sofa that caused the muscle spasm," she suggested. "Maybe you should get a professional massage."

"You're doing just fine," he assured her. "Please feel free to continue."

"If you insist," she said lightly.

She unbuttoned the top two buttons of his sport shirt so she could slip her hands underneath to massage his bare chest. She was concentrating on the sensation of his flexing pecs under her naked palm when she felt his hand cup her knee. She'd changed from the slacks suit she'd worn earlier into heavy jeans and a long-sleeve shirt, but his touch was as erotic as if her leg had been bare. She stepped forward, bending her knee slightly to make it more accessible, and he moved his hand slowly upward.

The sinew in her leg twitched, and she had to force herself to stand still as his thumb rubbed up and down a small area on the inside of her thigh. Deciding to play his game, she let her hands slide seductively down his chest until they were stopped by his belt.

His belly muscles clenched, and he drew in his breath and shifted in his chair. She was aware of his heart pounding as he stroked upward on her leg. She shivered, and without her knowing quite how he did it, he reached back, tumbled her onto his lap, and cradled her in his arms.

She put her arms around his neck, and he grabbed the gripper on her waistband with his free hand, pulling both it and her zipper open with one yank. He slid his hand inside her jeans and, with a little help from her, pushed them down and off. Her silk panties covered little, and this time when he put his hand on her thigh, it was flesh to pulsating flesh as his unruly fingers crept closer to their goal.

Her trained inclination was to resist, but her natural instinct was to plead for more, and more, until he finally touched her and set her aflame.

She clasped his shoulders and squirmed in his lap, eliciting a moan from deep in his throat as he moved to brush his knuckles against her dampness. Stunned, she cried out and shivered with exaltation.

Quickly he withdrew his hand and blinked. "Eve. What's the matter, sweetheart? Did I hurt you?"

It took her a moment to come back down to earth, and then she cursed herself for a fool. She should have been on guard and expected something like that after all she'd heard and read about passion.

"No, not at all," she whispered. "It just felt so..." She decided to go with the truth. "So good! Don't stop now."

"You know you're driving me crazy, don't you." His voice was raspy with need. "Shall we go in the bedroom?"

"Yes. Oh, yes," she whispered, and blew into his ear. Her good sense had vanished and so had her resolution not to let this happen.

He put his arms under her knees and stood, then carried her into her room.

While he stripped down to his underwear, she took off her shoes and pulled back the covers. Out of the corner of her eye, she saw him reach into the wallet he'd put on the lamp table and pull out a square foil packet. She silently blessed him for his thoughtfulness—even while her mind also registered the fact that he looked absolutely fantastic in his briefs.

Had she really done that to him, or was he always this...*ready* when he was excited? She fervently hoped it was the former.

Her fingers trembled as she reached up to undo the top button of her blouse, but he stopped her. "No, let me," he said, and set about the task.

The buttons were small, but even so he seemed unusually clumsy for a man of his age and experience. His hand kept falling to her breast. Finally she put hers over his. "Why don't you let me do it?"

He slid his out from under hers and looked at her wryly. "I guess you'd better. My hands are shaking so bad, I'll never get the thing off you."

Him, too? Was he as eager as she was? She hoped so!

She completed the task and slid the garment off her shoulders, letting it fall to the floor. But when she felt the cool air on her bare flesh, she was suddenly stricken with shyness. What if he compared her to other women he'd made love to—and found her wanting? She knew she was not nearly as beautiful as Bambi, and she didn't have any idea how to do the things that titillated men and brought them to climax.

Subconsciously, she averted her eyes and crossed her arms over her chest as she felt a crimson flush stain her face. What was the matter with her? She wore bikini bathing suits every summer that were skimpier than the bra and panties she had on now.

Gray was eyeing her admiringly, and he had no doubt seen many naked women. She'd been told often that she was beautiful, but no man had ever seen her nude.

"Eve," Gray said tentatively. "What's the matter? Are you cold?"

He reached out, gathered her in his arms and held her close. She could hear her teeth chattering.

"You're shivering," he murmured, and nuzzled her temple as he rubbed the bare flesh of her back and arms to warm her.

"I—I'm sorry," she apologized, desperate to keep him with her, but not knowing how to explain her strange behavior. She couldn't even explain it to herself. "I guess it's a chill. It is kind of cool in here."

Now she'd said the wrong thing again. It definitely was not "cool" in here. In fact, not more than a few minutes ago, they'd both been heated to the point of meltdown.

"Honey, are you afraid of me?" Gray's tone was gentle but probing.

She cuddled even closer in his arms. "Oh, darling, no! I could never be afraid of you. I love you."

She bit her lip. No, she mustn't say that. Gray didn't want her to love him.

"I—I want you," she amended.

He didn't react to her declaration of love, but asked another question. "Do you trust me?"

"Implicitly."

"All right then, here's what we're going to do," he told her. "Do you have a heavy robe?"

She nodded. "Yes. It's in the closet."

"I'll get it for you, and I want you to put it on and climb into bed, while I get dressed and go to the kitchen to warm up the tea. Then I'll bring you a cup and we'll talk. Okay?"

No, it wasn't okay, but it was better than having him walk out and never look back.

"That's fine," she said, then almost cried out with torment when he released her and walked over to the closet to get her robe.

He dressed quickly and left the room, while she slipped into her robe and climbed into bed.

He returned in just a few minutes with a cup of hot tea, which he set on the bedside table. Then he plumped up her pillows and helped her to sit up with her back against the headboard.

When he had her settled, he sat down on the side of the bed, then picked up the cup and saucer and handed them to her. "Here, try this. It's hot, but I don't think it will burn your mouth. It's more effective to treat a chill from the inside than the outside."

Eve felt like a wayward child who needed to be taken care of, and she hated it. Gray had all the dependents he could handle; she didn't want to be added to the list. She wanted to take care of him, not the other way around.

She lowered her gaze and drank the tea all in one gulp, then handed the cup and saucer back to him. "You're right, I do feel warmer now."

He took the dishes and put them back on the night

chest. "Good. Do you want to lie back down and cuddle up under the blankets, or—"

Her heart jumped with joy. "Do you mean cuddle up with you?" The question was out before she could reel it back in.

For a moment his expression brightened, and she was almost sure he was going to say yes, but then the glow faded and a look of sadness replaced it.

"Not today, sweetheart," he said tenderly. "There are some things we need to know about each other first. Our feelings have been getting way out of hand."

Again she felt the crushing blow of disappointment. "I know all I need to about you," she insisted. "What is it about me that's bothering you?"

A small smile lifted the corners of his mouth. "I don't believe 'bothering' is the right word. Maybe 'concern' is better."

He picked up one of her hands and held it. "Eve, I'm going to ask you a question, and I want a straight, no-nonsense answer. You mustn't lie to me or evade the issue. Understood?"

She frowned. "I wouldn't ever lie to you, Gray. You should know that without asking."

He squeezed her hand. "I do, but I had to ask. Please, don't be mad."

She squeezed back. "You're forgiven. Now, what do you want to know?"

He threaded the fingers of his other hand through her tangled curls. "Are you a virgin?"

Chapter Nine

Eve knew that she was looking right at Gray, but she didn't see him. She also knew her mouth was open, her jaw slack, but there was nothing she could do about it.

Well, so much for her attempt at projecting the worldly, sophisticated, suave woman who would be all the things a man of Gray's age and experience expected in a lover. She couldn't lie to him. Not only had she promised not to, but she'd never be able to carry it off. All he had to do was get a little physical with her, and she soared all the way to the stars and back without even waiting for him.

Then she'd frozen up and treated him as if she were an untouchable angel who didn't even know how babies were made. You can't get much more amateurish than that, she thought.

The sound of his voice jarred her back. "Eve, answer me. You promised you would, and I have to know. Have you ever...been with a man before?"

She hung her head. "No, I haven't, I'm sorry—"

"Sorry!" he exclaimed. "What do you have to be sorry about?"

"I'm sorry I'm such a disappointment. I led you on and then freaked out at the last minute."

He put his fingers under her chin and lifted her face. "And why did you do that?" At least he didn't seem to be mad.

She couldn't avoid looking at him. He had her head angled so that her gaze merged with his. "I don't know. I—I didn't mean to. I wanted to make love with you, but something just paralyzed me. Oh, Gray, I'm so ashamed."

A low moan escaped from his throat and he wrapped her tenderly in his arms. "I'm the one who is ashamed. I had no business getting involved with you, no matter how strong my own feelings were. I've known all along you were too young. You're hardly more than a kid—"

She pulled away and glared at him. "I knew you were going to say that, and it's not true. I'm twenty-four years old, well-educated, and support myself. I've been dating boys and men since I was fifteen, and I'm a virgin by choice, not because I've been locked up in a convent."

Eve detected the amused half smile on Gray's face before it disappeared. "I don't doubt that for a minute," he said, and gathered her to him again. "I can feel for all those guys you've been turning away, even though the thought of anyone else touching you, intimately or not, makes my blood boil."

"Then what's the problem?" she asked. "Don't you want me anymore, now that you know I'm not as experienced as the other women you've known—in the biblical sense, that is."

His arms tightened around her. "Of course, I want you. I suspect I'll never get over wanting you, but I'm not a cradle robber—"

She reared back once more. "Now don't start that again," she warned angrily.

He caught her by the shoulders and held her in place. "Eve, I'm thirty-six years old, a middle-aged man. I've been married, divorced, and have an eight-year-old daughter. I'd never forgive myself if I robbed you of your innocence."

"I told you, I'm not all that innocent," she insisted. "I know what goes on between a man and a woman. Just because I haven't experienced it yet, doesn't make me untouched."

He loosened his hold on her shoulders, and caressed them gently. "It makes you special," he murmured softly. "It means you've been saving yourself for that one special man in your life, preferably your husband."

"Now you sound like my dad," she grated, then immediately regretted it.

"That's because your dad and I are more or less of the same generation," he explained. "I'm certainly old enough to be your uncle, if not your father."

"But why is that so important to you?" she asked, still not understanding. "As long as we want each other, what difference does age make?"

"The problem is that all I'm willing to promise you is a loving but uncommitted relationship that either of us can walk away from at any time," he pointed out. "But you want marriage and children and happy ever after."

It irritated her that he seemed to be able to read her mind. "What makes you think you know what I want?" she snapped.

He smiled sadly. "Sweetheart, the very fact that you haven't been willing to have sex with the men you were attracted to is a dead giveaway. You must have been up against a lot of pressure to put out. If I violated you, your trust, just because I have the hots for you, then later walked away and left you with nothing—no children, no security—I'd be damned by my own selfishness. I can't do that to either of us, Eve.''

"So are you saying you don't want to see me anymore?"

"Not 'don't want,' but 'don't dare.' There's no way I could think of you as a sister, or as just another date. It's better that we don't see each other socially, but we'll run into each other now and then. After all, we'll be working together on the school roofing project once it gets off the ground.''

"And Tinker? Don't you want me to tutor her anymore?"

He frowned. "Ah, yes, Tinker. I'd forgotten about that complication."

He was thoughtful for a moment, then asked. "Will you give me a few days to think about it? I doubt she'll be up to studying this week, anyway."

This conversation was becoming painful for Eve; her head began to ache. After all, he was right about one thing. She didn't have to apologize for her virginity, and she wasn't going to again. If he thought she wasn't experienced enough to satisfy him, he was probably right.

"Take as much time as you want," she said. "But I'd appreciate it if you'd not give Tinker the impression that I would just quit because I didn't want to work with her anymore. That could be very damaging—"

"Honey, I'd never do that," he assured her. "Now, is there anything you need before I leave?"

Yes—you, here in my bed loving me.

"No, nothing," she said, and scooted down so she was lying flat. "Would you please turn off the light in the kitchen when you go out?"

"Sure." He leaned down and kissed her softly on the cheek. "Good night."

She curled up in a tight ball under the covers, and listened while he flipped off the kitchen light, then shut the front door that locked automatically behind him.

It was only then that she released the gush of tears and let them soak her pillow.

Eve didn't hear from Gray again, and as the days went by she suspected he was intent on breaking all ties with her, including her tutorial relationship with his daughter. She'd called the hospital on Tuesday to ask about Tinker, and had been told that the girl had been released, so at least Eve knew the youngster was healing and no longer needed constant medical supervision.

Still, Eve was apprehensive about Tinker's well-being. Had Gray taken her home to his house from the hospital, or had he backed down and let Bambi have their daughter part-time again?

Eve didn't trust Bambi, and was pretty sure Gray didn't either. But some women could wrap men around their little fingers and seduce them into giving them anything they wanted. She suspected Bambi was one of those.

Eve had been watching Gray's weathercasts, and knew he hadn't missed a day. She remembered that he'd told her he had a cousin who could baby-sit Tinker for a couple of weeks. So the fact that he was working didn't necessarily mean Bambi had Tinker. But had he found someone to replace his cousin?

The phone rang early Saturday morning, and to Eve's joyful surprise it was Tinker. "Daddy and I are going over to Mount Rushmore and we want you to come along. Please," Tinker said, getting right to the point.

Eve's insides melted, and her whole being longed to accept the invitation. But she suspected this was Tinker's idea, not Gray's.

"Honey, does your daddy know about this?" she asked.

"Sure," Tinker answered. "He said it was okay. We're gonna take a picnic an' everything."

After the way they'd parted last, and then all this time without a word from him, Eve found it difficult to believe Gray would invite her to spend the day with him and his daughter.

"Let me speak to your daddy," Eve said. She had to know that he approved.

She could hear Tinker call to Gray and tell him that Eve wanted to talk to him.

"Hello, Eve." His tone was husky.

"Hello, Gray," she answered. "Were you aware of what Tinker was talking to me about?"

He cleared his throat. "Yes. She wants you to come to Mount Rushmore with us."

"Do you want me, too?" She wasn't aware of the double meaning until the words were out of her mouth.

"That's a loaded question, love," he rasped, "and the answer is yes—no matter which way you take it. Besides, I need to talk to you."

"Well, if you're sure, I'd love to go. What time will you pick me up? Do you want me to bring something for the picnic?"

"Just yourself, and we'll be there in about an hour. Is that too soon?"

How could it be too soon, when she hadn't been near him for a whole week and was desperate for the sight of him? "No, that's fine," she assured him, and hung up.

It was a beautiful June morning, bright and warm with

sunlight. Eve was tempted to wear shorts, but that would
be too obviously seductive. She didn't want Gray to think
that she was teasing him, deliberately tempting him to do
or say things he didn't want to.

No, she wasn't going to throw herself at him ever again.
If he didn't care enough for her to marry her, it would be
folly to force him into making that commitment by stir-
ring up his testosterone beyond his ability to resist. He'd
always feel trapped, and she'd always feel guilty.

Instead, she wore red jeans and a red-and-white striped
T-shirt with white sneakers, and tied her black hair back
with a white scarf.

She'd just finished her makeup when the doorbell rang.
Her heart started to pound and her stomach muscles
clenched as she hurried to the door and opened it.

She drew in her breath as she stood face to face with
Gray. Either of them could have reached out and caressed
the other. She could have walked into his arms, and she
knew he would have hugged her to him. He could have
sauntered into the house, swooped her up in his embrace
and carried her to the bedroom, and she wouldn't have
protested. But neither of them acted on their feelings.

For a few minutes they just stood there looking at each
other, and it was Gray who finally spoke. "You're very
beautiful." His tone was low and vibrant.

"So are you," she murmured, then realized men aren't
called "beautiful." "That is—you're a very handsome
man." she amended, embarrassed.

He was wearing blue jeans and a gray T-shirt, but no
matter what he wore—suits, slacks or jeans—he always
looked fabulous.

She was still struggling to regain her composure when
she realized something was missing. "Where's Tinker?"

She poked her head out the door to look up and down the balcony.

"She's in the car," he said. "I wanted to talk to you for a minute alone."

Her curiosity was aroused, and she stepped back. "Won't you come inside?"

He shook his head. "No, this will just take a minute. Eve, I'd like you to continue tutoring Tinker."

She was delighted and opened her mouth to tell him so, but he hurried on before she could. "You've been doing such a great job, and she wants you. So far I've let her think it was because of her injury that the lessons have been suspended, but she's eager to start again Monday. That is, if it's all right with you."

"I'd be happy to go on working with her, Gray," she assured him. "But are you sure...? That is, you said—"

"I know what I said," he interrupted, "and it still stands. It will be extremely difficult for me to be in the same house with you and not touch you, but I should be able to control myself for a couple of hours a day, five days a week.

"Besides, I won't be there very often. I need to spend more time at the station tracking the weather and keeping up-to-date on new equipment. I promise I won't get in your way."

She wondered if he knew just how badly she wanted him to get in her way—to be around all the time, to tease her, to love her.

"Okay then," she said as lightly as she could manage. She closed and locked the door. "We'd better be on our way."

A short while later they approached the tiny community of Keystone, which was not only the gateway to the Mt.

Rushmore Monument, but a rugged historical mining town in its own right.

As Gray concentrated on navigating the corkscrew road to the top of Iron Mountain, Eve and Tinker enjoyed the stunning views through the rocks and trees.

"My class at school came here once last year," Tinker said, "but it was boooring."

Surrounded by all this natural beauty, Eve found that hard to believe. She never failed to find it thrilling. "Why was it boring, honey? The heads of the presidents is one of the largest pieces of sculpture ever created. You're very fortunate to live in its shadow and to be able to see it whenever you want to."

Tinker shrugged. "But people already know about them. Why do we have to study them?"

Eve smiled. "I suppose that's true of the folks who live around here, but to most of the people in the world, carving gigantic faces out of stone on the side of a mountain is an astounding project. Millions of tourists come from thousands of miles away to see it."

Tinker looked at her wide-eyed. "Really?"

"Yes, really," Eve assured her. "A famous sculptor named Gutzon Borglum was chosen to carve the heads—"

Tinker laughed. "That's a funny name."

"Not funny," Eve corrected her gently, "just different from the ones you're used to. It took him almost twenty years to complete it."

"How did he get up there?" Tinker asked. "And how did he keep from falling off?"

Eve looked beseechingly at Gray, and he picked up his cue without hesitation. "It was done with machinery, honey. Tall cranes with seats that the workers were strapped into so they had both hands free to work on the faces.''

Tinker wrinkled her nose in puzzlement. "What workers? You said that man with the funny name made the faces.''

Gray raised his eyebrows at Eve in a gesture of frustration, but forged ahead. "Mr. Borglum was the man who drew up plans for the heads and figured out how to carve them, but he had helpers who did the actual blasting and chiseling," Gray said carefully.

They spent the rest of the morning viewing a film about the sculpting of the faces and exploring the national monument. They had a slight change of plans at noon, because both Gray and Eve had forgotten that there was no picnicking allowed within the memorial grounds, but there was a restaurant with a spectacular view of the heads and they had lunch there.

In the afternoon, they took a ride on one of America's last steam trains: the 1889 train. Old Baldwin engines and 19th-century coaches provided a two-hour trip along a route that miners and pioneers used to explore the Black Hills.

Eve was tired but happy when Gray brought her back to her apartment, but then things got awkward. Gray insisted on walking her to her door, but it was raining hard and neither of them wanted Tinker to get wet. Obviously he wouldn't come in and leave Tinker in the car. But Eve wondered if he would kiss her good-night. That seemed highly unlikely. Would they shake hands? That idea bordered on the absurd considering their degree of intimacy the last time they were together.

Gray seemed as unprepared to handle the situation as she, and they finally ended up making a mad dash to her door, thanking each other for a great time, and saying good-night...without touching.

During the following week, Eve went to Gray's house every afternoon to tutor Tinker, but she saw him only to say "hello" and "goodbye." The rest of the time he was holed up in his office, unless he was interrupted by business errands.

It was frustrating and beginning to wear on her nerves. She felt like an untouchable who was to be avoided except when she was performing her assigned duties, then she was to leave as quickly as possible.

Tinker offered quite a bit of unsolicited information, such as that she was still living with her dad, and that Gray and Bambi "yelled at each other a lot." What a strained atmosphere for a little girl to have to endure, Eve thought.

Meanwhile Gray was going through his own brand of hell. By far, the worst was his estrangement from Eve. It was torture to have her in his house for a couple of hours a day and not be able to acknowledge her presence.

And Bambi was being especially uncooperative and obnoxious. It started when she discovered that he really had reduced her spousal support. Although both he and his lawyer had told her he was going to, she apparently hadn't believed he'd do it until that day she'd called him at his office.

Bambi called the house every day and talked to Tinker, but when she asked for Gray, he always found an excuse not to talk to her. Then she started calling him at the station when she knew he'd be there, but he'd asked the operator not to put her through. He managed to avoid her until Friday, when she rang the station and told the operator it was an emergency.

The operator told Gray, and he immediately thought of Tinker. Had something happened to her that her babysitter couldn't handle?

He had the call put through. There was no way he could avoid it. "What's the matter, Bambi? Is Tinker all right?"

"How would I know?" she snapped. "You won't let me near her. Honestly, Gray, if you cared just a fraction as much for me as you do for your precious daughter, our marriage never would have broken up."

That was truer than she could even imagine, he thought as he fought back his smoldering ire. She'd deliberately used his love for Tinker again to get what she wanted from him.

"You said there was an emergency, so what's happened?" he grated.

"You know very well what's happened." The little girl tone of her voice was gone, replaced by grown-up rage. "I tried to use my credit card to buy a dress at Suzanne's, and the store wouldn't accept it. They said my name had been taken off it or some such nonsense. Just what in hell are you up to?"

"I'm not up to anything, Bambi," he said quietly. "I told you that I'd no longer pay you as much spousal support. That includes access to my credit cards. After our divorce, I was no longer compelled to let you use them, but as long as you didn't run up big bills I didn't take your name off them. I have now, though. The ones you have are invalid. You'll have to apply for your own, if you want some."

"But I can't," she wailed. "I don't have enough income."

"Then go to work like the rest of us, and earn your

own support," he said sharply. "You're a smart woman. You worked and made a decent income before we were married. There's no reason why you can't do it again."

"You're just being hateful," she said on a sob. "You know I can't hold down a job. I have a daughter to look after."

He took a deep breath. So she was deliberately ignoring the fact that he intended to sue for full custody of Tinker. Well, he wasn't going to get into that now.

The sobs didn't go unnoticed by him, either, but he was surprised to realize that he was no longer affected by them. He'd seen and heard them often enough to know that she could turn them on and off at will.

"That is no longer applicable," he told her. "But even if it were, millions of women all over the country handle the twin jobs of working and raising their children."

"Well, I'm not 'millions of women,'" she said indignantly. "And don't threaten again to take Tinker away from me."

"I'm not threatening you with anything," Gray said, trying to sound reasonable, but getting more and more exasperated. "I'm stating a fact. My lawyer is having the papers drawn up now, and next week we're filing for full-time custody of Tinker."

"Your daughter!" she screeched into the phone. "She's my daughter, too, and if you think I'm going to sit around and let you take her away from me, you're sadly mistaken."

For a moment he was too angry to speak, and before he could get himself under control, Bambi continued.

"It's that woman, isn't it. Eve! Boy, is she aptly named. Is she promising you Paradise? Well, just make sure she doesn't lure you into eating any apples!"

Bambi slammed down the phone, leaving Gray sputtering in frustrated rage.

Chapter Ten

The following morning, Saturday, Eve was curled up on the sofa, watching the national all-day news station and sipping her first mug of coffee for the day, when the phone rang.

It was Gray, and her heart flipped, sending her nerves into spasm. "Eve, I'm in a bind and I need help," he said apologetically. "Is there any chance Tinker and I could come over and discuss it with you?"

She couldn't imagine how she could help him, but she'd do her best. "Of course, Gray," she assured him. "You know you're always welcome. The coffeepot's full, and I'll fix cocoa for Tinker."

"Good. I'll stop by a bakery and get doughnuts." His voice softened. "I knew I could count on you."

He hung up before she could answer.

By the time she'd straightened the apartment and changed into a newer pair of jeans, Gray and Tinker were ringing her bell. She opened the door, and the aroma of freshly made doughnuts preceded them into the room.

"Oooh, they smell so good," she moaned, and rubbed her stomach. Tinker giggled.

Gray grinned and handed her the box. "I think they're still warm, so have at 'em. I'll pour the coffee."

Eve took the container and arranged its contents on a tray, which she carried into the living room and set on the coffee table. "Well, this is a treat. It isn't every day that I have guests for breakfast who bring their own food."

Gray walked in behind her with the coffee and cocoa and mugs on another tray, which he set on the floor; her coffee table wasn't big enough to hold two large trays. The three of them got down on the floor beside it and sat cross-legged, while he poured the beverages into mugs and handed them out.

Eve noticed that he'd maneuvered to get the table between him and her, and Tinker sat next to her.

"Help yourselves to the doughnuts," he said, and reached for a puffy sugar one, which he placed on a paper napkin. Tinker chose a pink-frosted cake type, and Eve took the one with chocolate frosting and nuts.

For a few minutes they just concentrated on eating. Eve loved sitting on the floor. It was so informal and relaxing. It felt to her as if they were a real family gathered for snack time.

When Gray finished his doughnut, he wiped his hands with a clean napkin and looked at Eve. "I noticed you have a TV set in your bedroom. Do you mind if Tinker watches it while we talk?"

Eve swallowed. "Not at all."

"Aw, Daddy," Tinker protested. "Why can't I stay here with you guys? I won't tell Mom what you talk about."

Gray looked as startled as Eve felt. "When have I ever

asked you not to tell your mother anything I've done or said?'' he asked.

Tinker lowered her head. ''Well, never, I guess. But she's always asking me what's going on at your house, who comes over and what you do and say. I...I don't always tell her—''

Her voice broke, and Eve couldn't resist the urge to put her arms around the child and pull her close. She could see that Gray was too incensed with Bambi to deal with the situation yet, and he had a right to be. It was wrong of Bambi to put their little girl in the middle of their problems.

''It's okay, Tinker,'' Eve murmured as she cradled Gray's daughter to her. ''I don't even know what he wants to talk to me about, but he probably thinks it's something that would be boring for you. You'd be more apt to enjoy some of the Saturday morning television shows.''

Tinker sniffled. ''But now he's mad at me.''

''I'm not mad at you, sweetheart,'' Gray assured her as he lifted the coffee table and put it down on the other side of him. He moved over and sat close to Eve and Tinker.

''Your mother has probably told you I want you to live with me all the time,'' he continued, ''but I'm having trouble arranging for someone to come to the house so early in the morning and be with you until I get home from the station. That's what I want to talk to Eve about. Maybe she knows other teachers who don't teach in the summertime, need the extra money and don't mind the odd hours.''

Eve's eyes widened. So he hadn't found a baby-sitter yet, and his cousin was probably leaving to join other members of her family. What would he do if he couldn't find anyone? Would he have to give in and let Bambi have Tinker part-time again, after all?

"I can't think of anyone right offhand," she said to Gray, "but I know a lot of teachers. I'd be happy to get on the phone and talk to the ones I think might be interested."

He ran his fingers through his hair. "I hate to bother you with my troubles, but I'm at my wits' end. I've run out of time. I've contacted everyone I know, but the hours are so impossible, and I need someone starting Monday—"

"Daddy, why can't Eve take care of me?" Tinker piped up. "She doesn't teach school in the summer, and she comes to our house every afternoon to tutor me, anyway. She could just stay with us all the time."

Out of the mouths of babes, Eve thought as she fought back the rising tide of both elation and foreboding that threatened to consume her. That would be a really explosive situation. She wondered which of them would climb into the other's bed first.

Gray's face was as flushed as she knew hers was, and neither of them could meet the other's gaze.

Gray finally found his voice. "Honey, that's just not possible. Eve has her own home to take care of—"

"Then she could go home when you get off work and come back again at bedtime like cousin Leona did," Tinker persisted.

"We can't impose on Eve—" he began.

"What does *impose* mean?" Tinker interrupted.

By this time Eve's mind was whirling. Desperate needs took desperate measures, and Gray's need was desperate. Eve wasn't going to let him lose his bid for full custody of his daughter just because she was a virgin. Big deal! You'd think that qualified her for sainthood, when all it meant was that she'd never met a man who she wanted to be her first lover.

That is, not until Gray came along.

Now his innate sense of honor and decency might cost him his child. No way was she going to allow that.

Father and daughter were still bickering, but Eve had lost track of the conversation, so she cut in. "Gray," she said, but he apparently didn't hear her, so she touched his bent knee. That got his attention.

"Gray, I don't think you should be so quick to discount Tinker's suggestion."

He looked at her as if she were spouting gibberish. "What are you talking about? You know why it's out of the question."

"I know there's no other choice," she reminded him. "I—"

She stopped and looked at Tinker, who was still sitting on the floor beside her, all ears. "Tinker, I'd really like to talk to your dad alone for a few minutes. Would you mind dreadfully?"

Tinker smiled. "Are you going to talk him into letting you baby-sit me?"

Eve chuckled. "I'll try my best, but in order to work my magic, I have to be alone with him. My bedroom's down that short hallway—" she pointed in the right direction "—you know how to operate the TV."

Tinker giggled. "Okay," she said, then stood up and scampered off.

Gray glared at Eve. "And just what magic is that? Are you planning to cast some kind of spell over me?"

"Do you think I could?" she asked softly.

"I know damn well you could," he admitted. "And so do you, so let's cut the nonsense and get right to the point. Do you actually want to baby-sit Tinker?"

"I'd be happy to," she said. "We get along well together, and it would make tutoring her much easier. I can do it in snatches all day instead of trying to cram it all into a couple of hours.''

"But you're deliberately sidestepping the crucial point, and you know it," he said grumpily. "In the first place, I don't have an extra bedroom. I use the third one as an office.''

"No problem," she countered. "Tinker has a set of twin beds in her room. I don't think she'd mind sharing the second one with me. If she does, I can sleep on the sofa in the office.''

"Like hell you can," he roared. "It's too uncomfortable. Besides, I can't have you sleeping in my house and in the room next to mine. I'd never get any rest. Have you any idea how tormenting it is for a man to want a woman as much as I want you, and know he can't have her?''

Her gaze meshed with his. "Have I ever resisted you when you came on to me?" Her tone was low and loving.

He reached out and cradled her to him. "No, you haven't," he groaned. "And that's why I can't agree to your baby-sitting Tinker.''

He held her gently, but she could feel his heartbeat speed up when she put her hand on his chest. "If you'd fend me off, tell me I'm too old, or too far behind the times to appeal to you, I could leave you alone. I'd never pester you with my attentions. But you're so sweet and willing. It drives me crazy to know you want me, too. I'm supposed to be the mature, responsible one in this duo, but I'd never withstand the temptation of knowing you were sleeping in the room right next to me.''

She wound her arms around his neck and rubbed her cheek against his. "Then you know how I feel. It's just as hard for me. It would be so easy for us to seduce each other, so why don't we? After all, we're two consenting adults.''

He stroked her breast, and she shivered with delight. "Yes," he agreed, "but I've been an adult a whole lot longer than you. I'm the one who's supposed to be keeping my cool. Besides, in the long run it wouldn't do any good. Since we're not married, we couldn't sleep together in my house as long as Tinker is there. I won't set that kind of an example for her.''

Eve winced. She felt as if she'd been slapped, although she knew he hadn't meant it that way. No wonder he thought of her as a child. She was acting like one, greedily reaching out for what she wanted, with no thought of what it might mean to others.

Gray was determined to set a good precedent for his impressionable daughter, and all she, Eve, cared about was her own selfish desires.

She pulled out of his embrace and scooted a few inches away. "You're right, of course," she said somewhat testily, "and I promise you, I won't let that happen.''

He looked puzzled by her change of tone and attitude and started to speak. "Eve...?''

She stood and looked down at him. He seemed less intimidating that way. "However, you still need a babysitter, and I'm still available, so why don't we try this arrangement for a while? I'll spend the nights at your house and stay there with Tinker until you get home in the early afternoon. Then I'll leave and come back at bedtime to start the routine over again. On weekends, of course, I'll stay here in my own home.''

He frowned and stood up, too, but she hurried on before he could say anything. "During this time you'll still be searching for a housekeeper, or whatever it is you have in mind. So I won't have to be there too long—''

"Eve!" He didn't raise his voice, but his tone was commanding. "What's the matter? Did I say something wrong? If I did, I didn't mean to."

Her resentment drained away. She couldn't take out her disgust with her own behavior on him. He had enough problems without her adding to them.

"No, Gray," she assured him. "You didn't say anything wrong. You're always a gentleman. I'm the one who needs reprimanding now and then."

She saw the puzzlement in his expression and quickly changed the subject. "Why don't you take the rest of the day to think this over, and let me know tomorrow what you decide? I'll understand either way."

He reached for her and took her in his arms again. "I don't need time to think it over," he said huskily as he rubbed his cheek in her hair. "I want you with me, and we'll take it one day at a time."

Eve packed a weekender case on Sunday evening with the few personal items and clothing she'd need for her stay at Gray's house. She moved into Tinker's room, and Tinker was delighted; the extra twin bed was a little confining, but comfortable.

The first few days were both exciting and awkward. Exciting, because Eve could now tutor Tinker during the morning hours when the child was well rested and receptive. Awkward, because Eve knew Gray usually went to bed early; his early morning work schedule was so demanding. She made it a point to arrive at his house shortly after the dinner hour, but he seemed to feel that he had to entertain her.

Instead of retiring for the night, he stayed up with her

to talk, read or watch television after Tinker was put to bed. Eve enjoyed it immensely, but on Wednesday, when she caught him nodding off in his lounge chair, she knew he really needed his sleep.

She walked over to wake him, putting her hand on his shoulder and shaking him gently. "Gray, go to bed."

He looked up at her with sleep-filled eyes, then grinned and pulled her down onto his lap. "Yes, Mama," he murmured, and cuddled her close.

She knew that she shouldn't allow this. They were playing with fire, but it felt so good. With Tinker in the house, there was no chance of it getting out of control. Gray wouldn't allow that. It was so nice, though, to curl up with him, lie back and let the enchantment between them flow.

She put her head on his shoulder, and he tenderly massaged her hip and outer thigh until, with a contented sigh, he fell back to sleep. She sat there for a while, continuing to revel in the gratification of loving him and the fantasy that he loved her, too.

She also nodded off, and when she surfaced again, the clock on the mantel told her it was almost midnight. Time for them both to be in bed. She tried to sit up, but his arms tightened around her and held her to him.

That would have been fine with her, but she knew he couldn't rest well with her sprawled all over him. The chair was comfortable enough for one person to sleep in, but not two. If she could just release herself, she could get up and cover him with a blanket before going to her bed in Tinker's room.

She breathed deeply and tried again, and once more his arms tightened around her. "No," he murmured sleepily.

She knew that he wasn't awake enough to know what was going on—only that he liked it the way it was.

Finally she raised her head and whispered in his ear. "Don't wake up, my darling. I'm only going to my bed."

She teased his earlobe with her tongue, then sucked it lightly. "Good night, sweetheart."

Without warning he moved his hands enough to cup her head on either side. "I love you so much," he murmured thickly as he brought her face down to his and gave her a kiss—one that was tender and filled with longing.

It lasted only a moment before his arms dropped to his sides and he was once more asleep.

For the last two days of that workweek, Eve wandered around in a daze. Gray hadn't mentioned the incident, and neither had she. Did he remember what had happened? There was no doubt that he was asleep both before and after, but how conscious was he during it?

Why would he say he loved her unless it was true?

He'd told her that he was never going to fall in love again after his disastrous marriage to Bambi. Knowing Gray, she was sure he meant it. On the other hand, people seldom had complete control over their passions. Could he have been expressing a deeply buried emotion that he didn't dare examine when he was fully awake?

Eve's free weekend started when Gray arrived home on Friday afternoon, and continued until Sunday evening— and she was happy to see this one come. It gave her a release from the tension she was always under when she was with Gray. Part of her hoped he'd find a housekeeper as soon as possible; the rest of her dreaded the moment when she'd no longer have even that tenuous connection to him.

On Saturday, she decided to give her tiny apartment a thorough spring housecleaning. While she was sorting through the drawers of her desk, she found a brochure from the University of Nebraska at Lincoln, telling of their new program to provide teachers with the classes necessary to qualify them to teach children with learning difficulties.

This subject had been her interest all along, but the University of South Dakota, where she'd received her BA, hadn't offered the extra training. She remembered now finding the brochure from Lincoln in the mail a few weeks ago. She'd put it in a drawer in the desk, intending to get back to it when she had a few minutes to spare. But then Gray and Tinker had charged into her life, and she'd forgotten all about it.

She stuffed the envelope back into the drawer, but made a mental note to remember what it was and where she'd filed it. It might give her an out someday—if she needed one.

That weekend Gray wandered around lost and lonely. He'd known that he'd miss Eve on the days she wasn't with him, but he hadn't had the faintest idea how much. They'd agreed to stay apart on Saturdays and Sundays when Gray was at home to take care of Tinker, and he'd tried to fill in the empty hours with things he and his daughter could do together—but to no avail.

Tinker missed her, too, and couldn't understand why Eve couldn't be included in their weekend activities. Gray made excuses, but they were weak and unconvincing.

As if that weren't enough, he was plagued by the dream he'd had the night he fell asleep in his chair. He wasn't prone to having erotic dreams, and this one wasn't actually erotic. It was sweet and tender and filled with unbearable longing.

The dream had neither a beginning nor an end, but at

some point during the night, he thought Eve had come to him and let him hold her while they slept. There had been no passion, but the all-consuming love he'd felt when they'd kissed went way beyond passion. It warmed his soul.

It's true that when he awoke the next morning he'd found that he'd slept in his chair all night, but that wasn't unusual. The chair was comfortable, and he sometimes dozed in it if he didn't go to bed early. Besides, Eve hadn't mentioned anything about nocturnal wanderings, and he wasn't going to embarrass her by telling her his fantasy.

He had another problem though—Bambi. Ever since Gray had taken Tinker to his house from the hospital and he had filed suit for full-time custody of their child, Bambi had been drowning him in letters, phone calls, legal actions, and everything else she could think of.

Gray managed to counter most of it, but it took up valuable time that he didn't have to spare.

She'd been livid when she found out that Eve was baby-sitting Tinker, and made all kinds of accusations. But since she couldn't prove that there was anything going on between them—for the simple reason that there wasn't anything—Gray threatened counter legal action, and Bambi backed down on that subject.

Gray hadn't told Eve about it because he knew it would upset her, and he was pretty sure that he could control Bambi.

It was no wonder that he had an aversion to marriage.

Gray took Tinker to church on Sunday morning, and in the Sunday School Department, they ran into Keith and Virginia Spenser and their daughter, Linda, who was Tinker's age. The Spensers lived just a few blocks from Gray, their children went to the same school, and Keith was a reporter at the TV station where Gray worked.

"Gray, we were hoping you'd be here this morning," Virginia said as the little girls ran off to their classroom. "I know it's spur of the moment, but Linda's birthday is next weekend and we'd planned to have a party for her then, but yesterday afternoon my mom, who lives in Denver, fell and broke her hip—"

"Oh, hey, I'm sorry," Gray said.

"Yeah, she has degenerative arthritis, so her bones are pretty brittle and break easily. She'll be in the hospital for several days, but when she's released, she'll need someone to take care of her. Linda and I are leaving the day after tomorrow, and I don't know when we'll be back, so Keith and I decided to have Linda's party tonight—if we can round up enough kids. Please, say Tinker can come?"

Gray hesitated. He knew his daughter didn't like going to parties. She wasn't really close friends with any of her group, and they teased her about her reading difficulty.

Still, he couldn't allow her to hide all her life. It was important that she learn how to mix and socialize. And how to stand up for herself. To give as good as she got.

"Of course, she can come," Gray said. "What time and where?"

Virginia's smile was dazzling. "Our house, five o'clock. A sleep-over. We'll swim first, have a barbecue, then go to a movie. Tomorrow morning we'll give them breakfast and take them home."

Tinker wasn't at all enthusiastic when Gray told her about it after church was out. "Oh, Dad," she whined. "I don't like to be with those kids. They're all smarter than me, and they love to tease me. I'd rather stay home with you and watch television. Or maybe you and me could go to a movie."

Gray knew that she wasn't telling the whole truth. She was a lonely child and desperately wanted to be accepted by her classmates and the neighborhood kids. But she'd been hurt too often by their insensitivity. Consequently, she had become too attached to Bambi and to him. They were her safe harbor: they loved her even if she couldn't read.

Gray took her out to brunch and talked her into going to the party, then tried to call Eve to tell her about the change of plans, but she wasn't home. He got her answering machine instead, so he left a message on it, telling her it wouldn't be necessary for her to come tonight.

He dropped the phone in its cradle and slumped in his chair. He should be elated to have a free night. He hadn't been out on a just-for-fun date in months, unless you counted the abbreviated trip to Deadwood with Eve, and that had ended in disaster. But now the thought of going out with any other woman left him cold. All he could think of was Eve, and how eagerly he'd been looking forward to having her back in his home, even though she couldn't be back in his arms.

He changed clothes and spent what was left of the afternoon taking care of some business that had been piling up on his desk. Then he took Tinker to the party. At six-thirty, he made himself a peanut butter sandwich and a scotch on the rocks, and settled down in front of the TV to watch the St. Louis Cardinals play the Chicago Cubs.

He never drank when he was responsible for Tinker, but tonight was going to be a long, lonely one, and a couple of drinks wouldn't hurt.

The Cardinals had just hit a home run when the doorbell rang. Because of the racket from all the cheering on the TV, he wasn't sure whether he'd heard something or not, but the second time he did hear it and got up to investigate.

He opened the door and stared. There on the step stood Eve, dressed in a long, red flowered tank top dress. With it she wore red sandals, and her ebony curls were somewhat tamed by a red chiffon scarf.

She looked amazing! Not that she didn't always, but something about this outfit hit him right in the libido, and took his breath away.

"E-Eve?" he stammered. "What are you doing here?"

She looked at him questioningly as she walked past him. "What do you mean, What am I doing here? I work here."

Her expression changed to concern. "Gray, are you all right? You look as if you weren't expecting me."

He shut the door behind him and followed her into the living room. "I *wasn't* expecting you," he said. "Didn't you get my message? I left one on your answering machine."

She groaned. "Oh, darn, I forgot to check it. I'm always doing that. I spent the day at a family reunion at my parents' house, and when I got back to the apartment, I didn't even think to check for messages. I'm sorry. Was it something important?"

"Only if you don't mind a wasted trip," he said, and seated her on the couch. He turned off the television, then sat down beside her and proceeded to tell her about Tinker's party.

"Did Tinker put up much of a fuss about going?" Eve asked when he'd finished.

He shook his head. "No, not really. She wasn't exactly happy about it, but she agreed without much argument. I wouldn't have made her go if she'd really been upset about it. The Spensers have a new swimming pool, and Tinker loves to swim.''

He grinned sheepishly. ''I guess you could say I bribed her. I bought her a new bathing suit to wear. She's also an excellent swimmer, so nobody will tease her about that.''

''Poor little kid,'' Eve said sadly. ''It pains me to think of her hurting. But she's catching up to her grade level fast. By fall, she probably won't need any more tutoring, and then she can show those ornery kids how smart she really is.''

It warmed Gray's heart to hear Eve defend his daughter so vigorously. How much happier his life would have been if he'd married Eve instead of Bambi, he thought. But, of course, that would have been out of the question, even if he'd known her. She was a child at the time—not much older than Tinker was now.

What more proof did he need that he was too old for her!

Eve fidgeted. ''Well, since you won't need me tonight, I'd better get on home—''

He couldn't bear to let her go so soon, and, unable to resist, he put his arm around her shoulders. He was careful not to touch any part of her that he shouldn't. ''No, not yet,'' he murmured. ''I've missed you. Stay for a while.''

She didn't rebuff his gesture, but neither did she snuggle. ''Are you sure that's what you want?''

''Oh, yes, very sure. It might not be the smartest thing to do, but it's definitely what I want.''

He felt her relax a little, and he kissed the top of her head. Her hair was as fragrant as an English garden bouquet, and he gently rubbed his face in it. It tickled his nose and sent little pinpricks down his spine.

''May I get you a drink? Maybe some chips and dip?''

he asked reluctantly, hoping she'd say no. He didn't want to release her and take the chance that she wouldn't let him this close to her again.

"No, thank you," she said on a sigh, and relaxed even more.

They weren't touching intimately or carrying on a titillating conversation, but nevertheless Gray was becoming aroused, and fast. Damn, he'd never had this much trouble controlling his sex drive before. Sure Eve was beautiful, but he'd known a lot of beautiful women. Especially in his business. She was also sexy, but again, in the TV industry he met a lot of sexy women. So why did she leave him reeling?

He nuzzled her warm, fragrant neck, and she shivered and burrowed closer, this time completely relaxed. The temptation was too great, and he lowered his arm to her waist and cupped her breast with his other hand. With a moan, she turned toward him and wrapped her arms around his neck.

He turned, too, and pressed her chest against his, but still he couldn't get enough of her. As he slid his hand down the curvaceous rise of her firm hip to rest on her knee, the silky smoothness of her dress was like an aphrodisiac. It enflamed his senses, and all his good intentions turned to ashes. His palm rubbed slowly back up her leg, bunching the skirt of the garment and taking it along.

Her legs were bare, the skin smooth, and he was in agony. It was all he could do not to take her right here and now. He knew she wouldn't resist, and the only thing that stopped him was the knowledge that she was a virgin. What kind of man would he be if he took what she was offering? The problem was that he couldn't seem to stop.

Before he could get his wits about him, he realized that

Eve was unfastening his shirt. He should stop her, he knew, but he didn't. Instead he helped her.

"Eve, I want you," he groaned as he tore off his shirt, and she unsnapped his jeans.

"I know," she said. Then she unzipped his zipper, an act that was nearly his undoing—in more ways than one. "I want you, too. There's nothing wrong with that."

"I hope not," he said as he reached behind her and unzipped the long zipper on the back of her dress. "Because this time we've gone too far. I can't stop."

"Me, neither," she murmured, and slipped her arms from her unfastened dress.

Through the haze that clouded Gray's mind, he thought he heard a slight noise coming from somewhere in the house, but he knew the doors and windows were locked and he was too steeped in bliss to think about anything but Eve—

Then a loud gasp filled the air, and Bambi's strident voice rang out loud and clear. "How dare you make love with this woman in plain sight, with my little girl right down the hall! And you call me a bad mother! I'll see you both in hell before I let you have custody of Tinker ever again! You'll be lucky if you get visitation rights!"

Chapter Eleven

Eve lay frozen on the couch, nude to the waist, her skirt pulled up to mid-thigh, and unable to see or feel or even think clearly. Gray had bolted off the couch to face Bambi, and Eve heard them shouting at each other, but couldn't tell what they were saying. All she knew was that one minute she was soaring on the verge of ecstasy, and the next she was plunged into a black hole.

Gray and Bambi were so engrossed in their argument that they weren't paying any attention to her, and she took the opportunity to grab her dress and pull it up to her chin, then roll off the couch and scramble across the room.

When she got to the fireplace, she zipped the back of her dress as high as she could quickly reach, then stumbled blindly to the door. She scooped up her purse from the hall table, and ran.

Her hands shook as she worked to unlock her car door and turn on the ignition, but all she could think of was getting away from there. As she backed down the driveway, her car ran over part of Gray's beautifully manicured lawn, and when she came to the street she turned without making any conscious decision as to which way to go.

Eve wasn't sure how long she drove around aimlessly before her mind began to function again. When it did, she fervently wished it hadn't. She'd never been so humiliated in her life! Just thinking about it made her break out in a cold sweat.

Not that she didn't deserve it. Gray had been up-front with her from the start. He knew his ex-wife, knew what she was capable of, and knew he was tied to her because of their daughter. But had Eve had the good sense to listen? No! She'd been so sure that she knew more than he did about what he wanted.

By now it was dark, and she didn't know where she was. There had been a lot of construction going on in Rapid City the past few years, and she wasn't familiar with all the residential areas anymore. She knew she wasn't anywhere near her apartment or her family home.

Not that she could go there, anyway. She wished she could throw herself in her parents' arms and let them soothe her and take away the embarrassment and pain. But she couldn't share this experience with anyone, least of all her mom and dad.

But neither could she go to her own apartment. Gray would come looking for her, and she couldn't face him, either. No, what she had to do was get away for a few days, try to sort out her tangled life and her options.

She felt guilty about abandoning her job as Tinker's baby-sitter and tutor, but Gray and his family were no longer her responsibility. They never had been, but she hadn't had the good sense to admit it.

It was Saturday of the following weekend before Eve had all her plans made, and felt strong enough to face her parents and Gray and tell them. Meanwhile, she'd been staying at her family's rustic summer cabin in the woods.

She'd called her mother to tell her that she and Gray had had a disagreement, and let her parents know where she was staying. She asked her mother not to tell him or anyone else where she was, should anyone come looking for her. She knew her secret was safe. Her mother was a wise lady. She'd taught her daughters to make their own decisions, and then let them follow those decisions without interference.

Now Eve was back home in her apartment again. She'd had lunch with her parents, and they had told her that Gray Flint had called every day to ask if Eve was all right, and would she be home soon. Of course, they couldn't tell him when she'd be back because they didn't know.

Eve was sorry that she'd caused him to worry, but it couldn't be helped. She hadn't known herself when she was coming back.

Eve had filled her parents in on her plans for the future. She assured them that she and Gray could never be more than friends because there were too many obstacles in the way of a romantic relationship.

Her parents had been supportive, as always, and her dad promised to honor his word to furnish all the materials for the new school roof at cost, even though she wouldn't be teaching there anymore.

Later that afternoon, when Eve was cleaning out her kitchen cupboards and putting the food in boxes to take to her parents' house, the phone rang. It was Gray.

"Eve! Where have you been? I've been going out of my mind—"

"I'm sorry, Gray," she interrupted, "but I just couldn't face anybody."

"No, I'm the one who's sorry, Eve. Look, I'm coming over. Please, wait there for me. We have to talk."

Gray hung up before she could answer, and he was on her balcony ringing the doorbell in record time. She'd been pacing the floor, eager to see him, but dreading it, too. Now she hurried to open the door. For a moment they just looked at each other, then Gray broke the silence. "Eve..."

He put out his hand as if to touch her, but she backed away and stood aside. "Come in, Gray," she said. Her knees shook, but her voice was steady. "I'm sorry I left so abruptly without giving you notice. Have you found a baby-sitter for Tinker?"

He shook his head. "No. I've gone back to my original arrangement with Bambi. I hated to do it, but she understands that it's just until you come back."

She turned and walked across the room to the sofa, knowing he would follow her. "Please, sit down. I have something to tell you."

Gray was pretty sure that he didn't want to hear what she was going to say, but he did as she told him. Eve seated herself in the upholstered chair across the small room from him. "No, honey, let me go first," he said. "There are no words to tell you how sorry I am about that episode with Bambi last weekend. I had no idea—"

"I understand," Eve interrupted. "And if it was the fault of either of us, it was mine. You warned me, but I wouldn't listen."

He was puzzled. "What do you mean I 'warned' you? I didn't know she would—"

"No," she corrected. "I mean you said you could never fall in love again, and that even if you did, you wouldn't consider another marriage. You told me like it was, but I wouldn't listen."

Damn him and his big mouth. He'd apparently been clumsy about telling her how things were with him. He hadn't meant to insult her or hurt her feelings. "Sweetheart—"

She put up her hand to silence him. "I'm not blaming you for anything, but I've come to realize that I can't live on the periphery of your life—"

"That's nonsense!" This time it was he who interrupted. "You're as much a part of my life as—as…"

"As Bambi and Tinker? No way. And what's more, I never will be. I'll always be the third angle of a triangle to you. The one you go to after you're sure the other two have been taken care of. You're a caregiver, Gray, and that's admirable in the extreme. But I didn't come along in time to be high enough on your list of people to care for."

She shivered and hugged herself. "I'm sorry, but I can't play third fiddle in your orchestrated priorities."

Gray felt as if he'd been poleaxed. He glanced over at her. She looked so desirable in her blue shorts and shirt set, but there was something wrong with the picture. She sat all huddled up, with her arms across her chest and her bare feet planted squarely on the floor. He ached to go over and take her in his arms, but it was as though there was an invisible wall around her posted with Keep Away signs.

He was almost afraid to question her, afraid of what she might say. She had good reason to be upset because he knew just how badly she'd been hurt. But he couldn't stand to have her so…so inaccessible.

"Eve, I know how shocked and humiliated you were when Bambi barged in on us the other day. I was, too, but I've taken steps to make sure that never happens again."

"I don't want to hear it, Gray. I only agreed to see you to tell you I'm moving."

He waited a few seconds for her to go on, but she didn't.

"Moving?" he asked. "What's the matter? Don't you like this apartment? I can't think why you wouldn't. It's comfortable and convenient."

"No, Gray, you don't understand," she said, and sat up straight. "I'm moving to Lincoln, Nebraska."

"Nebraska? You mean you're going to visit someone in Lincoln?"

She shook her head. "No, I'm leaving Rapid City to relocate, at least for the next year, in Lincoln."

He tried to gather his shattered concentration. There must be something he was missing, something he should have picked up on, but didn't. "But why? Have you had a falling out with your family?"

"No, my darling," she said sadly. "I've had a falling out with you. I can't live this way any longer. I was raised with a different set of values. I want a husband and children, and I want my husband to love me unconditionally."

Gray tried to assimilate what Eve was saying. This must be some kind of joke she was playing on him, but that couldn't be. Eve wasn't a cruel person, she'd never torment him like this; she was sweet and loving and kind.

"You aren't offering me any of that," she continued. "But for some reason I love you anyhow. I know the only way I can break up with you and make it stick is to move away, so that's what I'm going to do. I'm enrolling at the University of Nebraska to get the credentials that will qualify me to teach children with learning disabilities in the public schools."

"When?" Surely he could talk her out of this madness before she actually put her plan into action.

"As soon as possible," she said, and he noticed her voice was unsteady, too. "Certainly by the end of next week, and I'd appreciate it if you'd leave now, and not get in touch with me again."

"Eve, you can't mean that," he blurted. "At least give us a chance to work this out. I can't even fathom life without you."

He could see this was no time to try to reason with her. It would be better to wait a few days until they were both calmer.

He stood and looked down at her. "All right, I'll leave," he said softly. "But I'll be back. You can't dismiss me that easily. I love you too much to let you just walk out of my life—"

Eve gasped and looked stunned.

"What?" Gray said, startled. "What did I say?"

"You...you've never told me you loved me before." Her voice was only slightly above a whisper.

"I must have," he insisted, but now he was almost certain he hadn't. He'd become so used to denying his deeper feelings for her that they'd sneaked up on him without his acknowledging them.

Well, he could fix that quickly enough. He put his arms around her before she could protest, and held her close. "Sweetheart, if I haven't told you how much I love you, then I'm sorry, but how could you not know? I can hardly bear to let you out of my sight. And when we're together, I can't keep my hands off you. You're the beat of my heart, the joy of my life."

She felt him nuzzle her neck and, still in shock from his declaration of love, Eve surrendered to his embrace and let herself listen to his impassioned words. She loved and needed him, too, so why was it so difficult for them to get together and live happily ever after?

Actually, she knew the answer, had always known it. But she didn't want to face it right now. She wanted to stay encircled by his arms for the next few minutes and pretend that everything was all right. That all obstacles had been removed, now that he'd faced the fact that he loved her and had told her so.

"I won't ask you to take me at my word," he murmured against her ear. "I'll prove it. Marry me, Eve, and I'll do my best to make you happy."

Once more, shock bolted through her and her body stiffened. There they were—the magic words. *Marry me!* Only they weren't magic anymore. They had come too late. If he'd asked her before she had told him she was moving away, she'd have said yes and been ecstatic, but now it was too much like emotional blackmail.

Now that he'd admitted his love for her, she couldn't do that to him. It would put her in the same class as Bambi. As time went on, they'd both grow bitter; he would have been forced into a marriage he hadn't wanted, and she would know that he'd married her because it was the only way they could have sex without guilt.

She strengthened her resolve and pushed away from him. "No, Gray, it's too late for that now. You were right all along. You don't want a wife—you already have a family. And I want to get my special education teaching credentials."

She walked to the door and opened it. "Thank you for the proposal. I'm truly sorry I can't accept, and, please, be kind when you tell Tinker why I didn't come to see her before I left."

It struck the next morning while Eve was brushing her teeth. That funny tickle, like a cool breeze blowing across her nape, that invariably forecast a change in the weather. After all these years, it was so familiar that she seldom paid attention to it, unless it became a full-blown headache.

Speaking of full-blown aches, the one she was suffering from now was an ache in her heart. When she'd told Gray she was moving to Nebraska, she hadn't counted on him telling her that he loved her and wanted to marry her. That really shocked her. She'd tossed and turned and finally paced the floor all night pondering it.

But torment over Gray wasn't all she suffered from. As the hours went by, the tingle in her nape escalated, demanding to be recognized. Fortunately the national weather forecasts were for unsettled conditions, too, so there was no reason for her to mention her premonition to anybody. It was getting colder and cloudy, but that wasn't unusual for this time of year.

She hadn't heard from Gray since she'd sent him away, but she hadn't expected to. She had plenty of things to prepare to leave; she was too busy to brood. That is, until she finally crawled into bed that night. Then the anguish started, and she lay awake for hours.

The next morning, Monday, Eve tuned in to Gray's five o'clock forecast. She couldn't sleep, and she needed the sound of his voice even if she couldn't have the touch of his hand.

To her surprise, he was predicting a warmer trend with temperatures up from the past few days. But that didn't coincide with her quirky neck. As sharp as it was, he should be forecasting rain and wind.

Her first impulse was to call him, but then she backed off. No, she wasn't going through that again. She'd been rebuffed altogether too often by forecasters, even though it later turned out she was usually right. She was going to ignore the whole thing and not say anything to anybody.

The forecast at noon was for clear skies and warm temperatures, but her neck disagreed. It was still muttering *storm*. Again she was tempted to call Gray, but she wanted so badly to see him, talk to him, that now she wasn't sure that she wasn't exaggerating the discomfort in her nape as an excuse to get in touch.

She couldn't do that. Not after telling him she didn't want to see him or hear from him again.

The minute she woke the following day, Eve knew Rapid City was in for a great deal of upheaval weatherwise. Her nape not only tingled, it was in absolute turmoil.

It had never been this strong. Her neck was so stiff that she could hardly turn her head, and pain branched out into her shoulders.

She struggled out of bed and went over to look out the window. The sky was overcast, and the trees bowed in the wind. Possibly torrential rain? She wouldn't be surprised—there wouldn't be anything unusual about that at this time of year.

Ten minutes under a brisk warm shower left her feeling better. She was able to ignore the disturbance in her nape as she dressed and fixed breakfast, turning on the radio that broadcast news and weather continuously.

Today the forecast was for wind and overcast skies in the morning, with clearing in the afternoon. That was not what her neck said, but should she call Gray and tell him? She knew he wouldn't give any credence to her neck twinges. After all, what did she know? He was the meteorologist who got paid for knowing what was going to happen next, and even she had to admit that her predictions weren't always right.

Still, she wasn't going to take a chance. She couldn't be responsible for property damage and people being injured if a storm of major proportions hit, and she'd done nothing to alert the population.

She picked up the phone and dialed Gray's number at the station. "Gray, this is Eve," she said when he answered.

"Eve!" He sounded relieved. "Oh, sweetheart, I've been hoping you'd call—"

"Please, listen, Gray," she interrupted. "This isn't about that. I—I think you should know we're going to have a storm later today," she said hesitantly. "A bad one."

He cleared his throat. "What are you talking about? There's a low coming through with unsettled weather conditions, but nothing to worry about. You haven't been listening to my forecasts."

"But I have," she assured him, "and they're wrong. There's a storm headed for us, and it includes a lot of wind. I can't really say how I know." She hesitated a moment before continuing. "Some people say their arthritis acts up or their corn hurts when there's about to be a change in the weather, but I don't have any aches or pains. It's just a feeling...sort of a tingle at the back of my neck that alerts me. And the more intense the storm, the stronger the tingle. It's not always right on the button, but I'd say it's more accurate than your weather forecasting instruments.

"I know it sounds silly," she admitted, "but I woke this morning with the strongest sensation I've ever had, and it's getting stronger. Obviously, the weather bureau isn't picking it up, so I'm hoping you will alert the station and ask them to at least warn their listeners that a bad storm might be on the way.''

"Eve, I can't do that," he said. "Even with the most technical instruments, none of us is right all the time. I can't predict a storm based on the strength of a tingle in your neck.''

"I know that," she admitted. "But Gray, it's usually right.''

"Usually," he said sadly. "I'd do almost anything you asked, love, but 'usually' isn't strong enough for anything as major as issuing a storm warning. I'll promise you one thing, though. I'll keep an eye on the reports we get in here at the station, and if there are any changes, I'll do what I can to see they're broadcast immediately.''

Eve hung up. If Gray wouldn't help her, then she'd have to do what she could about getting the word out on her own. She glanced out the window. In just the past few minutes the storm had escalated. The wind had picked up, and it was raining.

Picking up the phone again she dialed her mother, told her the situation, and asked her to take the battery-operated radio and the portable telephone and go to the basement. She asked her mom to start calling everybody she knew and tell them there was a severe storm coming, and to take shelter immediately.

Her mother had had years of experience with Eve's weather predictions, and had learned not to question them.

Eve's second call was to Bambi's house. If Gray wouldn't take Eve seriously, then she had to at least make sure Tinker was safe. But she got a busy signal.

"Damn!" she muttered, and dialed the operator to ask for an emergency break-through, but she got no response.

Apparently, some of the telephone lines were down. The storm was vicious and it was approaching fast.

Eve put on her raincoat, grabbed her cell phone and her battery-operated radio, and rushed out the door. The wind whipped the rain, which in turn beat against Eve as she clutched the rail and fought her way down the stairs. She stopped first in the office to alert them and ask that they contact the other tenants in the building. To her great relief, the apartment manager said the first storm warning had just been broadcast over the radio.

It had been less than half an hour since she spoke to Gray on the phone.

Again Eve called Bambi's house, this time on her cell phone, but still she got a busy signal.

She hung up and debated whether to just go over to the house and make sure everything was all right, or to call Gray. She knew he'd be awfully busy tracking the storm now that it had finally made itself known, but on the other hand it was downright dangerous to be out in it.

Without further thought, she dialed Gray, but although she let the phone ring on and on, nobody answered.

That left Eve no other option but to go to the house herself, and make sure Bambi and Tinker were all right. Gray would never forgive himself if anything happened to them because he refused to believe they were in danger.

She gave a brief explanation to the apartment manager and then drove to Bambi's house. When she arrived, she ran up to the front door and turned the knob. It opened, but even before she stepped inside, she heard music blaring throughout the structure.

"Bambi!" she called as she glanced frantically around the room. There was no response, which wasn't surprising. She could barely hear herself over the noise.

"Bambi!" This time it was a yell, and at the same time she pulled the plug on the stereo.

"Hey, what's going on?" Bambi called from the back of the house. "Tinker, is that you? Turn that back on."

Eve found Bambi sitting at a table in the kitchen, polishing her nails, with the telephone to one ear.

Bambi looked up, surprised, as Eve stormed into the room. "What are you doing here—?"

"Hang up that phone!" Eve ordered, and even to herself she sounded furious and threatening.

Obviously Bambi thought so, too, because her eyes widened and she quickly did as she was told.

"Where's Tinker?" Eve asked.

Bambi looked bewildered. "I sent her to the store to get some diet cola and a Sweet Cherry lipstick to match my nail polish." She held out her hand. "See. Isn't it pretty? It's the latest color—"

Eve was furious. "Are you telling me you sent an eight-year-old child out to get diet cola and lipstick?"

Bambi's expression chilled. "Now look here, lady, don't go telling me how to raise my kid—"

"Which store?" she demanded.

Bambi backed down. "The…the supermarket on the corner of 48th and J streets," Bambi answered.

Eve gasped. "But that's at least eight blocks each way. When did she leave here?"

"Just a few minutes—" Bambi started to say, then glanced at the clock on the wall and jumped up. "Oh, darn, I didn't realize it was so late. Sandy called and we got to talking and—"

"Is there any chance Tinker's home now?" Eve interrupted.

Bambi shook her head, still looking bewildered. "I

don't think so. That is, if she is, I didn't hear her come in. But the music was kind of loud, and Sandy was talking..."

"For goodness' sake, stop chattering and listen to me," Eve said angrily. "What's the matter with you? How could you send your little girl out in a storm like this?"

Bambi blinked. "What storm? I didn't know it was storming—"

Just then a bolt of lightning followed by a crack of thunder silenced them both, and Bambi's look changed from bewilderment to terror. "Oh, no! My baby! Where's my baby?"

Chapter Twelve

Bambi started to run out of the room, but Eve caught her arm and kept her there. "Calm down and start acting like a responsible adult," Eve remonstrated. "I need your help. I'll search the house to see if Tinker's home, and you phone the store and ask if she's still there. Hurry, time could be crucial."

Eve searched every room, including the basement, all the while calling Tinker's name. Nothing.

"Any luck?" she asked Bambi when she got back to the kitchen.

"No, none," Bambi said as she hung up the phone. "They even paged her on the p.a. system, but she's not there. Oh, Eve, what am I going to do? Gray will be so mad when he finds out I sent Tinker out in this storm, but I didn't know it was this bad. We don't have to tell him, do we?"

Eve ground her teeth in frustration. The woman was more concerned about Gray's being mad at her than she was about their daughter's safety! Eve had never before understood just how scatterbrained Bambi really was. No wonder Gray stayed so close to them. He had good reason to worry about Tinker's well-being.

Eve swallowed the scathing words that threatened to tumble out, and concentrated on what had to be done. "Take your portable radio and go downstairs," she said, her tone defying argument. "Turn it on to the news, and if Tinker should come home, take her to the basement with you and stay there until I come back. Meanwhile, I'll look for her with the car."

Eve turned and ran out of the house. On the way to the car, a gust of wind and rain nearly knocked her over. Once in the vehicle, she started the motor and switched on the radio to find that every station was broadcasting severe storm warnings with tornado-force winds. The thick black clouds rumbled and spit long bolts of jagged lightning followed by claps of deafening thunder. Eve maintained a white-knuckled hold on the steering wheel as she pulled away from the curb and fought to keep the car in the right lane.

Frantically, Eve drove up one street and down the other, straining to see as sheets of rain slashed the windshield. All she saw was debris and tree limbs flying by; she felt the occasional jolt as some of it smashed against her car.

Eve shuddered and murmured prayers for Tinker's safety.

Then, when she'd almost given up all hope of keeping the vehicle on the street, she made one last turn. And there in the headlights she saw a small figure huddled under a large bush and clutching its trunk to keep from being blown away.

Eve slammed on her brakes and fought to open the door that was being held shut by the wind. She had managed to stop the car with the headlights still pointing at the bush. She pushed the door open and laboriously struggled to the shrub and put out her arm. "Here," she said to the still unidentified person who had her head down to protect her face from the driving wind and rain. "Grab my hand and hold on to it—tight."

"No!" said a small voice. "I'll blow away."

The noise of the wind made it difficult to hear, but she was almost sure it was a youngster. Eve raised her own voice. "No, you won't. I won't let you." She crawled closer until she could put her arms on either side of the figure—which on contact was readily identifiable as a child—and clutched the trunk of the bush with her hands. "What's your name?"

"Tinker," she said, and Eve felt dizzy with relief.

"Tinker, it's Eve. Put your arms around my neck and don't let go. There's enough weight between the two of us to ground us."

Eve wished she was as sure of that as she sounded, but thankfully Tinker trusted her and did as she was told. Eve reasoned that it would be easier to stay where they were and ride the storm out, but if those black roiling clouds put out funnels that reached the ground, it was imperative that they not be in the open.

Gingerly, she let go of the trunk and started using branches to help pull herself and Tinker up. It took almost superhuman strength, and the bush swept painfully back and forth across her unprotected face, but she finally accomplished it.

The next problem was to get to the car without being blown over. She tightened her grip on Tinker, and bent forward as she fought every step of the way to stay on her feet and head in the right direction.

Finally she reached the car, but the door had been

blown shut. Positioning Tinker between the vehicle and herself, she strained her body against the child's, and tugged at the door until she managed to get it open again. Then she pushed Tinker inside and followed her.

She hadn't turned off the motor, the lights, or the radio, and she put the car in gear immediately. Eve headed for Bambi's house. Thank goodness she'd found Tinker, but she couldn't bear to let herself think about Gray and the danger he might be in!

Driving in this wind was slow going, but eventually she reached her destination. She turned into the driveway as close as she could get to the house, then abandoned the car and, again with Tinker in her arms, fought her way against the elements to get inside the building.

Once she'd accomplished that, she tried to put the youngster down to stand on her own, but Tinker clutched at Eve, terrified.

"It's all right, baby," Eve said soothingly, at the same time trying to guide her to the door that led to the basement. "We're going downstairs until the storm is over. Give me your hand, and I'll help you."

Tinker was shaking. "Are we gonna get blown away?"

"Not now we're not," Eve said, sounding a lot more confident than she felt. "We'll go down to the basement and—"

As they got closer to the door, she heard two raised voices over the noise of the storm, coming from the bottom of the stairs. She knew one was Bambi. Could the other one be Gray?

The electric lines were down now, and the top two levels of the house were a dark gray, but the basement was even darker. As she and Tinker stood at the top of the stairs looking down, she could barely see anything, but she recognized Gray's voice and detected the fury and terror in it. She wasn't sure what he was saying, but it was directed at Bambi.

The storm was so loud, and they were so involved in their quarrel, that Eve couldn't get their attention. However, when she was a little girl her dad had taught her a sharp commanding whistle, and she put her fingers to her mouth and blew.

That silenced the combatants. "I have Tinker," she announced loudly. "She's right here at the top of the stairs with me, and she's soaking wet, but otherwise fine."

"Tinker!" It was Gray, and Eve could see his outline in the dark as he ran across the room.

Tinker pulled her hand out of Eve's and scampered down the steps. They met at the bottom, and Gray swept his daughter into his arms and hugged her, all the time muttering, "Thank you, thank you, thank you!"

From where Eve stood, she could see Bambi join Gray and Tinker in a loving family embrace, and she tried not to feel left out. She'd severed her tenuous ties with Gray. She had no business wishing he'd hug her, too. She was worried about her family, too, and hoped she'd have an equally loving reunion with them when this was over.

Straightening her spine, Eve started down the steps. "I'm sorry to interrupt," she said, "but we should get Tinker into something dry as quickly as possible. Bring me a blanket and some towels, while I get her out of these wet clothes."

Eve stepped off the bottom step and started to walk past Gray, but he reached out and grabbed her with one arm around her waist. Releasing Tinker to her mother, he put that arm around Eve, too, and held her close. He was as wet as she was.

"I love you," he said into her ear, "and it wasn't just

Tinker I was worried about. The fact that you could have been killed in this storm, too, was driving me crazy.''

He hugged her tight and kissed her hard, then disappeared up the stairs, leaving her shaken and off balance.

She managed to pull herself together, and eased Tinker away from Bambi, who was crying hysterically and being no help at all. Eve was helping Tinker take off her wet clothes and trying to reassure her, when Gray reappeared a few minutes later with towels and blankets. Eve dried Tinker off, and Gray folded a blanket in half and wrapped it around the child.

Eve had nothing dry to change in to herself, but her wet coat had protected the garments underneath to some extent. She removed the coat and towel-dried her hair enough to keep it from dripping in her face.

The wind howled overhead and the building shook above them, eliciting even more cries from Bambi. Eve looked around for something for them to crawl under, but Gray took command.

''There's a large workbench over on the right-hand wall,'' he said. ''It'll be crowded, but we can all get under it. Eve, take Tinker and follow me. Bambi, pull yourself together and get a move on.''

It was definitely crowded, but they all managed to huddle together on the concrete floor under the toolbench in the dark underground room. Before long, they could hear the tornado coming, like a freight train in the distance, rumbling closer all the time. Putting their arms around each other, they hung on as the noise escalated to a roar directly above them that shook the ground as well as the building.

It seemed to last for hours, but then it stopped, and there was no sound at all but Tinker's and Bambi's terrified sobs.

"I-Is it over?" Bambi stammered.

"Don't be too hasty," Gray warned. "It's not unheard of for these things to come in multiples, or this could be the eye of the storm. We don't want to survive one just to get caught in another."

The unnatural silence penetrated even further in Eve's mind, and another wave of fear stabbed her. What about her parents? Her sister, and other members of her family? She couldn't just sit there, she had to find out.

She was squeezed in between Gray and Bambi, and Gray had Tinker on his lap. Eve shifted and slid forward. "Gray, I'm going upstairs to see what's happening. I need to find out how my family is."

He crawled out and stood up. "Yes, of course you do. I'll go up with you and see how the weather looks."

They raced up the steps and found the house had been ravaged by the force of the winds and rain, but was still intact. The wet floor was strewn with broken glass and china, and they picked their way gingerly across it to look out a broken window. The sky was clear; there was no sign of more funnel clouds.

Gray went with her outside where the scene around them was chaotic. Rubble clogged the flooded streets and butted against the buildings; tree limbs, trash cans, bicycles, and cars were damaged and overturned. Eve was surprised to see her car had been spared anything more serious than a few deep body dents, although one parked at the curb was destroyed.

She kissed Gray goodbye, promised to drive carefully through the ruined streets, and headed for her family home. There, to her great relief, she found them all safe and sound. Both her parents' home and her apartment were out of the path of the twister, although they, too, had no electricity or phone service.

Back at her own apartment, after discarding her wet clothes, Eve took a hot shower and dressed in dry slacks and a sweatshirt. She was going back to Bambi's house. She couldn't get through on the telephone, and she was still worried about them. She'd left in such a hurry that she didn't even know if Gray's house had been damaged.

She hurried down the stairs and had almost reached her car when she heard an automobile turn into the driveway, and a voice shout, "Eve, wait. It's me, Gray."

Running footsteps crunched the gravel, and before she could recover from her surprise and respond, he caught her in his arms and crushed her against him.

"Gray! Oh Gray—" She was cut off when his mouth took possession of hers, and for a moment they were overwhelmed by relief and elation. Their hands roamed, their mouths ravaged, and their hearts hammered against each other's chests.

"Oh, Eve, my darling, my love," Gray murmured breathlessly against her throat as he nuzzled her sensitive skin. "I've been nearly out of my mind. I'm sorry I was so stubborn. I should have believed you and acted on your warning."

"No, sweetheart," Eve said. She put her hands on either side of his head and lifted it so she could rain kisses on his face. "You did nothing wrong. Nothing all the other weathercasters haven't done. I'm the one who's strange. Who knows? Maybe I'm a sorceress—"

He captured her roaming lips with his own, effectively silencing her. "If you are, then you're *my* sorceress," he growled before gently probing her lips apart with his tongue.

For a moment they were totally lost in the sweet agony of desire, as their deepening kiss sent waves of need through their trembling bodies.

Somewhere in the back of her mind, Eve knew they were standing in plain sight where anybody who walked by or looked out their window could see them—but it didn't matter. She was finally back in Gray's arms, and he was making it plain that he wanted her there. Nothing else mattered.

"I'm never going to let you out of my sight again," Gray eventually murmured, as Eve snuggled against him.

She loved it when he admitted his deep feelings for her, his fear for her safety, and his need to have her in his life. He still had responsibilities for his ex-wife and daughter, but she wasn't going to let those duties stand between them any longer.

"I'm glad to hear that," she said softly. "Does that include nights as well as days?"

She felt him stiffen. "That—that depends on you. What do you have in mind?"

"I'm accepting your proposal of marriage...if it still stands," she told him.

His arms tightened around her. "It does. When?"

She rubbed her cheek against his. "As soon as we can get a license. But you'll need a place to stay until then. You're—you're welcome to spend tonight at my apartment," Eve said. "I want you in my apartment, and in my life forever. We'll work out the problems with Bambi and Tinker as they come up."

Gray hugged Eve once more, then released her. "Then what are we waiting for?" he asked roguishly. "Let's go get them settled for the night so we can practice saying our wedding vows."

He took her hand, and together they headed for his car. "Oh, by the way, where were you going before I stopped you?"

"I was going back to Bambi's to make sure you were okay. Was your house damaged much?"

He shook his head. "It's the damndest thing. Bambi's had quite a lot of damage, but mine is just around the corner and it had none. Not even a cracked window or an uprooted shrub. Tornados are scary things. Totally unpredictable. Just like some women I know," he added, and squeezed her hand.

After fighting their way through wreckage-clogged streets, Gray and Eve finally made it to Bambi's house.

They found Bambi and Tinker cleaning up the rubble. Both were protectively dressed in blue jeans, sweatshirts, thick-soled athletic shoes and heavy work gloves. Bambi was sweeping the floor with a broom and brushing the jagged pieces of glass into a long-handled dustpan, while Tinker picked up the objects that had been thrown to the floor but not broken.

"I'm glad you came back," Bambi said. "We need to talk."

"I agree," Gray replied.

"Then we'd better sit in the family room," Bambi said. "There are no broken windows in there."

They followed her into the room, and Gray guided Eve to the sofa and sat her down beside him. Then he picked Tinker up and lifted her onto his lap. He talked reassuringly to her for a few minutes, then turned his attention to Bambi.

"My place has no damage, so we're going to take you and Tinker over there to spend the night," he told her. "You'll be safe there. Is that all right with you?"

Bambi looked from Gray to Eve, then back again. "Yes. I appreciate it," she said. "I really wouldn't feel very safe here."

"Good," Gray said heartily. "Then, if you'll throw a few things together that you'll need tonight, we can be on our way."

Bambi got up and left the room, but was back a few minutes later with an overnight case. Gray stood with Tinker in his arms, but Eve kept her seat, assuming she would be out of place if she tagged along.

When it became obvious that she was planning to stay there, Bambi said, "Eve, would you mind coming with us? There's something I want to say to you and Gray, but as you know—" she paused, then cut a glance at Tinker "—little pitchers have big ears, and besides it's past Tinker's bedtime."

Oh, dear, Eve thought. What now? Was Bambi going to put up a fuss about Gray and her spending the night together? Bambi might be flaky, but she wasn't stupid. She must know the strength of the magnetism between them and that after the tumult of this day nothing could keep them apart.

Reluctantly, Eve stood and picked up her purse as she followed them to Gray's car.

Once at Gray's house, he and Bambi got Tinker ready for bed and tucked her in, while Eve waited in the living room.

She shifted uncomfortably as she listened to the voices coming from Tinker's room. Eve could see now that she'd been all wrong about Bambi. Her helpless little-girl demeanor wasn't an act. She really was immature and incapable of assuming much responsibility. Gray knew that, and had done what he could to keep Tinker and her mother together by watching over both of them.

He was a loving father and a gentleman, and not many women were privileged to be loved by a man like that. And to think that she could have lost him tonight. Eve had had the scare of her life when the tornado struck. Gray could so easily have been killed—

Her thoughts were interrupted by Gray and Bambi coming down the hall. "Sorry to keep you waiting," Gray said as he walked across the room. He sat down on the sofa beside Eve, and took her hand in his.

Bambi took one of the upholstered chairs and got right to the point. "Eve, I—I don't have any idea how to thank you for saving my daughter's life—" Her voice trembled and broke.

Eve was aghast. "Bambi, that's not necessary—"

"Oh, I know you did it for Gray, not for me," she interrupted, "but—"

Eve slipped her hand from Gray's and sat up straight. "Bambi, you're wrong. I didn't save her—as you put it— for either you or Gray. I did it because I had to. I couldn't bear to think of that little girl out there in gale-force winds."

Bambi stood up. "Neither could I," she said, and began to pace. "But all I could do was cower in the basement and hide, while you and Gray were out looking for her. She could have been—"

Eve could see that the other woman was shivering and on the verge of hysteria. She stood up, followed by Gray, but she went to Bambi and put her arms around her while he held back.

It was more like embracing a child than an adult. Bambi was so slight, and she continued to tremble and bury her face against Eve.

"It's all right, Bambi," Eve murmured. "Tinker's safe and sound now, and no one's blaming you. If you had gone out of the house, *you'd* have been blown away. You were right to stay put."

"But...but it was my fault she was out in it in the first

place,'' Bambi sobbed. ''If I'd been paying attention to what was going on outside instead of talking on the phone and listening to loud music, she'd never have been in danger.''

Eve raised her head and glanced at Gray, who was standing in front of her but behind Bambi. He motioned and shrugged as if to say he either didn't know how, or didn't want to handle her. Eve took that to mean that she could do it her way and he'd go along.

''Bambi,'' she said gently but firmly. ''This tornado was a natural disaster that caught everyone by surprise.''

''But I should have—'' Bambi started to say something, but Eve interrupted her.

''*Should haves* don't count after the fact,'' she said. ''Just remember this experience and learn from it. Eight-year-old children need to be supervised and taken care of.''

Bambi squirmed out of Eve's arms, and reached into the back pocket of her jeans for a tissue to blow her nose. ''I know that,'' she said, ''but I'm not very good at it. I forget, or get involved in something else and don't pay attention…''

She was silent for a moment, then took a deep breath and went on. ''That's why I've decided to let Gray have full custody of Tinker. I didn't realize before just how oblivious I can be.''

Bambi's announcement took Eve completely by surprise, and she could tell from Gray's expression that it did him, too.

''Are you sure?'' he asked. ''I mean, couldn't you just try to be more observant?''

''I have tried,'' Bambi said sadly as she turned to look at Gray. ''But after a while I'm back to not paying attention again. I've had time to think about it during this long horrible day, and I'm not going to put my baby in danger anymore. I try to be a good mother, truly I do. But my mind keeps wandering, and pretty soon I'm in trouble again. If you want custody, Gray, I won't oppose you.''

Eve was dumbfounded. Bambi was voluntarily giving Gray full custody of their daughter. She'd never have believed it if she hadn't heard it herself.

The three of them were standing close together in the near darkness of the room, and Gray's glance traveled over his troubled ex-wife.

''We'll talk about this more tomorrow,'' he told her. ''Then we'll get together with our lawyer. Meanwhile, be absolutely sure you want to do it.''

''I am,'' she said, then looked at Eve. ''Eve, I owe you my baby's life. Just saying thank you will never be enough.''

Eve didn't want Bambi carrying that burden of guilt on her account, and was quick to say so. ''No, Bambi. You don't owe me a thing. There were mistakes made on all sides today, and we all three share in both the guilt and the glory. I feel especially blessed to be the first one to find Tinker, but I would call that a miracle—not an act of heroism.''

Later, when Gray and Eve had seen Bambi and Tinker settled for the night, they returned to Eve's apartment. The door had barely shut behind them when Gray took her in his arms and held her close.

''I seem to remember talk of a wedding before we left here a couple of hours ago,'' he murmured in her ear. ''Is that conversation still valid?''

She worried his earlobe with her tongue. ''Just try to get out of it,'' she said threateningly.

His arms tightened. "Not on your life. But are you sure? I can be awfully bossy at times, and once in a while I'm a real pain in the a—neck."

She nuzzled his throat. "I'd noticed. But don't forget I've had a lot of experience with pains in the neck, and I've learned to handle them pretty well."

He chuckled. "Seems to me the one today sort of got away from you."

She bit his lip. "Next time I'll know better how to handle a certain weather forecaster. But for now, are we going to stand around here chitchatting or—"

"No, ma'am, we are not!" he said. "We're going to turn in and get a good night's sleep, you in your own bed and me on the couch."

Eve blinked. "B-but I thought—"

He rubbed his cheek in her hair. "You thought I was going to try to get you to start sleeping with me now instead of waiting the few days until we can get married, but for me that's not an option."

Her head started to swim with confusion. What was he trying to tell her? Although they'd never had sex they'd been intimate enough at times to assure her there was nothing wrong with his libido.

"I...I don't understand," she said shakily. "Don't you want to make love with me?"

For a moment he stood perfectly still, then he took her by the upper arms and gently held her away from him so he could search her face.

"Eve," he said softly. "How could you ever think that? I've wanted you ever since the day I met you. You must know that. I haven't been very successful at controlling it."

Now she was even more puzzled. "Then why are you rejecting me?"

"Rejecting you!" His eyes widened. "Oh, sweetheart, I'm not rejecting you. You've waited all these years for the right man, and now you've chosen me. That's a precious gift, Eve, and I want my virgin fiancée to come to me on our wedding night as my virgin bride."

She felt tears of joy pool in her eyes as he gathered her to him and held her close. "I love you, my darling. Don't ever doubt that."

She snuggled against him and reveled in the warmth of his embrace. "I love you, too," she murmured against his chest. "Forever and forever."

*   *   *   *   *

THE **F RTUNES** of **TEXAS**

Membership in this family has its privileges
…and its price.
But what a fortune can't buy,
a true-bred Texas love is sure to bring!

Coming in October 1999…

The **Baby Pursuit**

by

LAURIE PAIGE

When the newest Fortune heir was kidnapped, the prominent family turned to Devin Kincaid to find the missing baby. The dedicated FBI agent never expected his investigation might lead him to the altar with society princess Vanessa Fortune.…

THE FORTUNES OF TEXAS continues with **Expecting… In Texas** by **Marie Ferrarella,** available in November 1999 from Silhouette Books.

Available at your favorite retail outlet.

Silhouette®

If you enjoyed what you just read,
then we've got an offer you can't resist!

Take 2 bestselling love stories FREE!

Plus get a FREE surprise gift!

Coming this September 1999 from SILHOUETTE BOOKS and bestselling author

RACHEL LEE

CONARD COUNTY:
Boots & Badges

Alicia Dreyfus—a desperate woman on the run—is about to discover that she *can* come home again...to Conard County. Along the way she meets the man of her dreams—and brings together three other couples, whose love blossoms beneath the bold Wyoming sky.

Enjoy four complete, **brand-new** stories in one extraordinary volume.

Available at your favorite retail outlet.

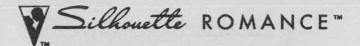

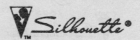

Silhouette ROMANCE™

VIRGIN BRIDES

**Your favorite authors
tell more heartwarming
stories of lovely brides
who discover love...
for the first time....**

July 1999 GLASS SLIPPER BRIDE
Arlene James (SR #1379)
Bodyguard Jack Keller had to protect innocent
Jillian Waltham—day and night. But when his assignment
became a matter of temporary marriage, would Jack's hardened
heart need protection...from Jillian, his glass slipper bride?

September 1999 MARRIED TO THE SHEIK
Carol Grace (SR #1391)
Assistant Emily Claybourne secretly loved her boss, and now Sheik
Ben Ali had finally asked her to marry him! But Ben was only
interested in a temporary union...until Emily started showing him
the joys of marriage—and love....

November 1999 THE PRINCESS AND THE COWBOY
Martha Shields (SR #1403)
When runaway Princess Josephene Francoeur needed a
short-term husband, cowboy Buck Buchanan was the perfect
choice. But to wed him, Josephene had to tell a *few* white lies,
which worked...until "Josie Freeheart" realized she wanted
to love her rugged cowboy groom forever!

Available at your favorite retail outlet.

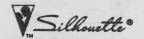